Unashamed

Leah Braemel

Published by Somerlane Publishing, 2022.

UNASHAMED

First edition. September 20, 2022.

ISBN: 979-8215551233

Written by Leah Braemel.

Also by Leah Braemel

Hauberk Protection
First Night
Private Property
Personal Protection
Deliberate Deceptions
Hidden Heat
Hauberk Protection: The Complete Series

Standalone
Unashamed
All I Need for Christmas

Watch for more at leahbraemel.com.

Chapter 1

The flare of light on the driveway drew Max's attention away from quartz countertop and undermount sink he was lowering onto the base cabinets. A thunk followed by his best friend and business partner's cursed "for fuck's sake, Moretti, you could have broken the damned slab," could probably be heard out in the yard. The flash had been caused by Hayley O'Connell—the owner of the house he and Noah were renovating—opening the back door of her Honda. He completely forgot about the countertop when Hayley leaned inside, giving Max a perfect view of her camo work pants tightening over a beautifully formed ass.

Man, she was brains and beauty wrapped in one perfect package. Where he'd gone straight into the trades after high school, Hayley had graduated from U of T with a degree in business economics. While working for one of the big banks down on Bay Street, she'd discovered she had a knack for choosing the right house to renovate and flip. Three years ago she'd ditched her high heels and pencil skirts for steel toed boots and a tool belt. Okay, so she didn't really wear a tool belt—that was entirely Max's fantasy—but for all the jobs he'd worked on with her over the past two years, she'd been on-site and totally hands-on for all the renovations, not afraid to pick up a hammer along with the rest of the crew.

Every single house she'd renovated sold for a comfortable profit. Then again, between her eye for renovations and the Toronto housing market, Max would bet his half of M&M Construction any house she touched would sell at a profit.

"Stop mackin' on my woman and hand me the damned number two Robertson, will ya?"

"Hey, I saw her first." Max handed Noah the green-handled screwdriver but found himself drawn back to watching the woman of both their dreams. "If she's anyone's woman, she's mine."

As much as both he and Noah had fantasized about her in the two years they'd known her, she had been dating someone else the entire time, which put her in the "hands-off" column as far as they were concerned. Then, four months ago, her investment banker boyfriend had been caught with his tongue down the throat of some chick at a Blue Jays' game—featured on the stadium's huge-ass video screen. The moment Hayley's Facebook status changed from *In a relationship* to *Single*, Max's hopes of dating her doubled.

She'd straightened, tucking a white hard-hat beneath one arm, and a bag of what were probably paint swatches and fabric samples in the other. Her shoulder-length blonde hair shone almost white under the late August sun, and her skin gleamed as sweat beaded on it now she was out of the car's A/C. The multiple layers of tank tops she wore clung to her curves. They would cling more once she came inside—the AC hadn't been hooked up and the house was at least ten degrees warmer than it was outside even with all the windows open.

"Why do women wear three layers of shirts like that?" he wondered aloud. "Especially when it's fuckin' hot out? How come one shirt isn't enough?"

"How am I supposed to know?" Noah cursed. "You gave me the wrong fuckin' driver, dickhead. Give me the red one. You know, the one I was using before your brains migrated down to your nutsac?"

Max exchanged screwdrivers with him and resumed his gawking.

A *Here comes the Bride* ringtone from Hayley's phone floated in through the open window. Max leaned on the counter, watching her answer it. She was a continual ball of energy even when she was just talking on the phone. There was always something moving—a hand brushing through her hair, her fingers drumming on the railing.

Shifting from foot to foot. Her speech was rapid fire, clipped, especially when she was pissed off. As she was now.

Noah humphed. "Hey, doofus, we're supposed to finish off this kitchen this week. It's going to take both of us to do that. So get your thumb outta your ass, will ya?" Noah continued with a bunch of other "still got the...to do" blah blah blahing that Max tuned out.

Max wasn't normally a slacker, but when Hayley was near, it was like all his hormonal inner teenager genes made an appearance. He'd stumble over words, his palms got sweaty, and he was getting damned tired of having to position himself behind wallboard or counters to hide the boner that immediately stood at attention around her.

She was single. So was he. He should ask her out. What was he waiting for? Because she'd just gotten out of a relationship and he didn't want to be the rebound date, that's why.

That Dipwad might have made her skittish about getting into another relationship was a frickin' chunk of rebar under his unmanicured fingernails. "Why do you think she stayed with Dipwad for so long?"

"If you love someone, you put up with a lot of shit." Noah slid from beneath the cabinet and joined him by the window. "If I ever see that bastard again, he's gonna need a nose job that requires a damned good plastic surgeon."

If Max ever saw Dipwad again, he'd need not only a plastic surgeon but an orthopedist because he'd come away with a lot more bones broken than his nose. Years of playing hockey as his team's enforcer had taught Max exactly how to inflict pain, not that he'd used that skill off the ice, but with Dipwad it was tempting.

Hayley stepped onto the porch which left her right in front of the kitchen window. Instead of continuing into the house, she dumped her packages on a pile of boxes and turned her back on the house, staring down the narrow road at the row of Victorian houses similar to hers. "Of course I'm going to be at the party on Friday night, Sophie."

Party? Friday night? Max wondered if she had a date. He quickly ran through a variety of ways he could ask her out for Friday without being obvious. "Do you think she'd go out with me?"

"You won't know unless you ask. Which I intend to do as soon as she gets off the phone." Noah tugged at his belt, as if adjusting it to hide a woody.

Shit. He had competition. Of the worst sort. "I don't stand a chance against you, do I?"

"Sure you do." Noah frowned. "But why does this have to be a competition?"

"Because it's Hayley O'Connell we're talking about." All he needed to add was the "duh." Sweet, gentle, lovable Hayley. The type of girl you could feel confident bringing home to introduce to your mother, not share with your best friend.

"What makes you think she won't choose you over me, doofus?" Noah cuffed the back of Max's head. "I was razzing you back there. I've seen the way she looks at you."

And Max had seen how Hayley eyed Noah. "Come on, I'm a first-generation Guido complete with big Catholic family who loves to interfere in every part of my life, not to mention my parents aren't competing in the richer-than-Trump marathon like yours. Oh, and then there's the whole man candy lottery you won. I mean, look at you" he waved toward Noah's head, "you have this whole sun-kissed blond hair, blue-eyed thing going on that the chicks all dig. And that stupid single dimple they all go gaga over."

"Geez, Moretti, women love dark-haired guys like you too. That's where the 'tall dark and dangerous' saying comes from—they think you're exotic."

Hello, how the hell did Noah think he qualified under the 'tall' part – dark and dangerous, sure, but tall? Give him a frickin' break.

Okay, yes, Max knew he wasn't bad looking. Years of working construction had built up his arm muscles and abs, but he was also aware that he was just under six feet in a world where women had wanted that "extra inch." And his family was definitely a dollar—make that a couple million—short when they compared bank accounts with Noah's father. Not that Noah had access to the family money anymore, but most women figured they'd be able to weasel their way back into Noah's father's pockets and then empty them.

"In case you forgot, doofus, you've dated twice as much as I have in the past year, so don't give me all this bullshit about women choosing me over you."

Part of the reason why he'd had to date twice as much was because most of the women he'd gone out with were looking at their long term strategy, which didn't include a guy with only a high school diploma and a job that relied upon a volatile real estate market. He'd figured out long ago that after meeting Noah and learning of his university diploma and family connections, most women shifted their focus and dumped his sorry ass, or used it to try to wheedle their way out of his bed and into Noah's.

Max stared out the window, craving the woman on the other side, her phone pressed to her ear, her forehead wrinkled at whatever Sophie was saying to her. How he longed to smooth those worries away, to cook dinner for her, and take her to bed, to prove to her she was the only woman who mattered in his world.

Noah shifted his belt again, making Max grimace in the knowledge his best friend was probably picturing a similar scenario.

Feeling magnanimous, he offered, "Look, she's gotta have a date for the party *and* one for the wedding reception next weekend, right? So how about I ask her to the party, and you take her to the wedding."

"You're just trying to get out of going to a wedding because you know women always cry at those things and you can't handle women crying."

"I grew up in a house with five women, shit-for-brains." Max rolled his eyes. "I know exactly how to handle tears. Unlike someone I know."

"I try not to make women cry in the first place."

"Moretti women don't need a reason to cry. They cry when they're sad, they cry when they're happy — Lucy," his youngest sister, "can cry at a freaking telephone commercial. I don't like weddings because every damned single woman starts eyeing you as they mentally plan their own wedding and realize they need a groom. I swear the wedding planners pump estrogen into the churches during the damned ceremony to drum up new business."

Noah rubbed his fingers together in a world's-smallest-violin gesture. "So ask Hayley out already, you big baby."

"You sure you won't get jealous if she says yes?"

Noah bawked like a chicken a couple of times.

Max flipped him off. Confident his plans were all set, Max picked up a rag and ran it over the counter to ensure they hadn't left any grease on it, humming to himself.

Two minutes later, Hayley's "Of course I've got a date" shattered Max's plans.

Shit. He'd waited too long.

HAYLEY ENDED THE CALL and frowned at the phone, though her frown was more for herself. *Why did you lie to her?* Which of course required the follow up, *why haven't you already asked someone to go with you? You've had four months to line someone up.*

Because you're out of touch with the dating scene, O'Connell. Time to get your act in gear.

Her phone rang again, the vibrations rousing her from her self-recrimination. Callie, Sophia's other best friend and maid of honor, who started the call with "So listen, I was thinking about the party tomorrow night."

Oh great. And so it began. Next Callie would say, "I've got the perfect guy in mind for you."

If she showed up alone, all her friends would be convinced she was heartbroken, or needed help to get back into the dating world by vying to be the one to find her the *perfect* man. When she already had the perfect man in her life. She glanced over her shoulder and confirmed that Max and Noah were in the kitchen. Make that the perfect *men*. When she'd been searching for contractors to help her renovate her first house flip, M&M Construction—Max Moretti and Noah McNaughton—had been repeatedly recommended. Not only did they do great work, they proved themselves time and time again to be courteous and reliable. And they were a treat for the eyes—especially when the weather was hot and they stripped off their shirts.

"If you haven't got a date already, I've got someone who would be perfect for you."

Yup, there it was.

"I told you, I've got someone in mind." Two someones actually. "Don't worry about trying to hook me up with anyone."

Max's smile had first caught her attention. Well, it had been *one* of the first things. His butt had been the first thing she'd noticed, considering he'd been facing away from her originally. When he'd turned around, and his cheek-splitting grin had delved right into her heart and spread roots. Then she'd met Noah and been zapped with a lightning bolt. And not just because the knob and tube wiring in the ancient 1930s townhouse arced when she had turned on a switch.

She'd been surprised she hadn't spontaneously combusted being in the same room as the two of them. It hadn't been her plan to be so hands-on during the renovations until she'd come to work on reno day and seen them in action. Max had that whole swarthy swagger about him, a pure testosterone package, while Noah tried to play it cool. She'd found herself entranced by the smack talk between them, amused by how they thought in sync, worked in sync. And then there were all those gorgeous muscles rippling as they ripped down plaster and wrestled appliances out of their way. Years of physical labor had made them worthy of a sculptor's chisel.

"But—"

"No, I want you to promise me—no blind dates, no sitting me beside a guy you think would be perfect for me, okay?"

"But Soph wants you to be as happy as she is. You know how she gets now she's a bride." Her tone turned wistful.

Not really. The ball-and-chain disguised by a white dress had never been her childhood dream like it had been Sophia's or Callie's. "I appreciate that you both worry about me, but I'm fine with the way things are."

"We just hate to think of you being all alone...Oh, did I tell you what Aiden's mother did this time? She asked Sophie what color balloons they wanted at the party. Balloons! Mrs. Demetrios just about had a shit fit and she was going on about how tacky it was. I swear she almost..."

Letting Callie ramble, Hayley studied the street, not seeing the ancient row houses she normally loved, not imagining the updates she'd do to number ninety eight if old Mrs. Morgan finally decided to sell. Instead she imagined herself in Max's arms, kissing him, and wouldn't you know it, Noah floated into her fantasy, his arms around her waist, nuzzling her neck, his erection hard against her behind.

"Look, I have to go. But don't worry about me, okay? I have a date for Friday." *Or I will if I play my cards right.*

She ended the call before Callie could wheedle the details out of her. Which would have been difficult considering she hadn't figured out whether to ask Max or Noah. Ah hell, why not just put the question out there and see who responded first? She shoved her phone back in her purse, picked up the swatches she'd dumped on the porch and headed inside.

Even though she'd chosen everything from the ceiling to floor, she couldn't stop her breath from catching seeing the finished product. Everything was perfect. And the kitchen? Totally worked. The black quartz countertop and black undercount sink accentuated the white cupboards. And she loved how the under-cabinet lights picked up the colors in the glass tiled backsplash.

She dumped her bags by the closet and walked to the kitchen, unable to stop herself from running a hand over the cool stone on the island. The kitchen was the last room to be finished. Which meant other than a few touch ups here and there, the renos were done and Max and Noah would have no reason to come back. Sure she had another house about to close, and an offer in on another, but it would be at least a month before she'd have a legitimate reason to see them again.

Max folded his arms and parked one hip against the counter he'd just installed. "You're frowning. You don't like it?"

"No, it's perfect. It's just how I envisioned it. This place is going to end up with a bidding war."

"Then what's wrong?"

How did she word this so it wasn't an obvious "I want to jump your bones" plea. Not that any guy she knew would object to that invitation, but this was Max and Noah. She wanted whatever could happen between either one of them to be more than a one and done. "I know it's short notice but are either of you free tomorrow night?"

"Why? What's doin'?" Noah mirrored Max's pose.

"I have to go to a friend's Jack and Jill party and I hate the thought of showing up alone. So I was wondering if either of you'd like to come with me. Be my date."

"Is Darrell going to be there?" Max practically growled, which sent tingles deep into her chest and down to parts that hadn't tingled in too long.

"Yes."

"So are you asking because you want to make that jerk jealous?" Max folded his arms across his chest, his full lips drawn into a scowl. "Or to give him a virtual middle finger?"

"Neither. I just want to stop all those inevitable blind dates my friends will try to set me up with if they think I'm alone."

Of course when she showed up with any guy, she'd face the other inevitable question single girls faced. The "so when are you getting married, dear" questions, which she'd definitely be asked if she showed up with either Max or Noah. And if she said they weren't serious, be they single or married, they'd totally view either man as fresh meat for some other unattached friend. "If you're not available, it's okay. I have a couple other guys I can ask."

Now there was a lie. Hayley hadn't been part of the dating scene for a while, and though she'd met a ton of guys through her renos, and had dozens of business cards as proof, most of them were married, or definitely weren't her type.

She held her breath as Max and Noah shared a look. She'd teased them before about having some sort of telepathic communication between them, but the way they were staring at each other, she could swear that they were having a conversation without saying a word.

After a long pause, and another long look between him and Noah, Max nodded slowly. "All right, I'll go with you to the party."

"It's sort of dressy. I mean, not tuxedo dressy, but not blue jeans either. Is that okay with you?"

"Don't worry. I've got a suit I can wear. I'll even shave." That beautiful big grin delivered a promise she couldn't wait to cash in.

What a pity. She loved that two day scruff he was currently sporting. "Thank you. It's down in the Distillery District." She loved wandering around the historical block with its reclaimed whisky distilleries that were now filled with boutiques and creative studios, not to mention its bars. "I can meet you there if you want."

Max shook his head. "Nope. I'll pick you up and we can go together."

"Good. Thanks"

"Then I'll be your date for the wedding."

Hayley started at Noah's statement, then saw the heat in his eyes.

"Don't worry. I clean up nice." Amusement crawled over his face, bringing out the single dimple in his right cheek that she had often wanted to kiss. "I own a couple suits too. Even own my own tuxedo."

"Great. Then I'm all set."

It was tough work, but Hayley was pleased that she managed to keep her satisfaction from her face. It took some effort, but she managed to walk out of the room as if things hadn't gone even better than she'd hoped. Once she was in the hall, out of sight of the two guys, she danced a little jig. Hot damn, she had not one date but two. With two very hot guys.

Life was looking pretty damned good.

Chapter 2

Whoever had chosen the Distillery District had made a good choice. Instead of being surrounded by lace and frou frou designs, he appreciated the limestone walls and timber and beam trusses and wondered if he'd ever get a chance to work on a similar renovation. The thirty foot ceilings of the hall swallowed much of the chatter, allowing Max to understand the MC as they called yet more numbers for the raffle tickets.

He'd never had to pay to attend a party before but Hayley explained the profits were going into a pot to be given to the bride and groom to put toward their honeymoon. Considering he didn't know anyone there, the party was a snorefest for him, but Hayley was enjoying herself and that's all that counted. Hell, Hayley could have insisted they attend an opera and he would have gladly followed her.

If anyone ever wanted to throw a shower for him and whoever he ended up with, he'd prefer to have a barbecue if it were in the summer, or at a hockey rink if it were in the winter, not some frickin artsy fartsy gallery, though this wasn't too bad on the Moretti Pretention Index. Still, why they couldn't have chosen the coffee bar or beer hall was beyond him. Considering the money they'd probably shelled out to rent this place, they should have just taken the dough to pay for some fancy-dancy vacation to Fiji instead of expecting the guests to shell out their hard-earned cash. As much as he'd love to give his bride (whoever she may be) such an exotic memory, he'd be damned if he'd expect others to pay for it.

At least Hayley had relented on the whole "meeting him here" suggestion and let him pick her up at her place. The anticipation of driving her home, walking her up to her steps, and planting a kiss on her—hopefully followed by an invitation inside—kept him happily occupied for most of the evening.

He sipped his drink, waiting patiently as Hayley talked with an older lady who was...who was she again? The groom's mother? No, the bride's. He'd gotten so used to seeing Hayley in her dusty work clothes and boots that he'd damned near swallowed his tongue when she'd opened the door earlier. Instead of having her hair pulled back in a ponytail, tonight her hair pinned up in some fancy do that she'd explained was a trial run for the wedding the following weekend. Even in the dim light of the hall, it shone like spun gold. Her white silk top had peek-a-boo lacy inserts along the sides that showed off her curves to perfection. He allowed his gaze to slide down over the curve of her ass and down to a pair of sparkly high heeled sandals.

He shifted, attempting to discreetly adjust the fabric currently strangling his dick. Man, he hoped she didn't want to stay too late. Anticipation was all very well, but he was going to end up with the world's worst case of blue balls soon.

Hayley touched the older woman's arm, and the two exchanged one of those air kiss moves that had always mystified him. When his mother met someone she liked enough to kiss on the cheek, you knew she'd kissed you.

"Sorry about that. Mrs. Demetrios was asking me about some mutual friends of ours and then she got on the subject of Sophia's wardrobe for the honeymoon and once she got started I couldn't get her stopped."

He liked Sophia, the bride-to-be, and he understood why Hayley liked her, but holy hell the bride's mother was one of those bridezilla types who had talked incessantly about the two bridal gowns she'd arranged for her daughter to wear, one for the wedding, one for the reception. Both of which were being held in Casa-freaking-Loma. If they weren't even leaving to go from one place to another, why the hell did she need two wedding dresses?

Max envied the easy way Hayley moved through the never-buy-domestic-cars-or-booze crowd. Not that he cared a damn what they thought of him, but he wondered if Noah might have been a better choice to accompany Hayley. Which perhaps she'd thought too when he'd offered to be her date. If he hadn't been watching her carefully, he might have missed how her eyes flickered to Noah before she'd nodded. And wondered again if there'd been a hint of disappointment within them.

Hayley sipped from the wine that Max thought was completely overpriced, and eyed him over the rim. "How long have you known Noah?"

Damn it, she was disappointed Noah hadn't asked first.

"Since high school—we went to the same boys' school." Her eyes widened in surprise when he named the school. "I got in because my mom worked a secretary there and finagled my tuition as part of her salary."

The upper-class kids had not accepted the 'scholarship candidate' as part of their ranks—all except Noah who hadn't cared how big Max's parents' bank account was. Or wasn't. It was only Noah's friendship that made him go back each day and not beg to be transferred back to the public school system.

"Why do you live together? I mean, he's *Charles McNaughton*'s son. He could afford to live wherever he wanted, but he stays with you."

"It's a long story, but his father got pissed off when Noah announced he wasn't planning on following dear old dad into the family business. Next thing Noah knows is his trust fund is cut off and his father's kicked him out of the family. So me and my family are all he has now."

The DJ changed from some fast rap number that no one could dance to and look dignified to Norah Jones' *Come Away with Me*. Talk about a perfect distraction. Max held out his hand. "Want to dance?"

Aware of heads turning to watch their path, he led her onto the teeny dance floor wedged between the tables. She felt right in his arms—her curves and valleys hitting all the right places.

Max rested his cheek on her hair and breathed in her scent—there was a hint of perfume, probably something expensive, but he liked it. It was subtle and spicy, which suited her perfectly. Between her scent and the way she snuggled against him as they danced, Little Max rose to the occasion. Great, just what he needed—the song would end and she'd pull away revealing his erection.

Dipwad was there, circling the fringes, eyeing Hayley. *Suck it, asshole. She dumped your sorry ass. And if I have anything to say about it, you don't get a do-over.*

The song ended too soon, replaced with yet another of those head-jamming numbers. *Yeah totally not making a fool of myself trying to dance to that.* Max led her off the dance floor. "Want another drink?"

"I'd love one."

"Why don't you go grab our seats and I'll bring it to you." Max headed to the bar where he asked for a glass of red wine for Hayley and given he'd had a Molson earlier and would be driving later, switched his order to a bottle of water, non-sparkling please.

When he returned to the table, he discovered the other couples they'd been seated with had disappeared, and the seat he'd previously claimed was now occupied by Dipwad himself.

Max hesitated, torn between wanting to protect Hayley and giving her privacy. Not that Darrell was threatening her at all but it bugged Max that he'd have the stones to go anywhere near her.

He jabbed a finger directly at Max, as if there was any doubt as to who he was talking about. "He's not your type, babe. Trust me. And when it's all over, no one will see you as someone they want to bring to their family. Not with the reputation you'll end up with."

While he wanted to get married one day, saw himself with kids, Max knew Brooks was right—Hayley was too good for him—but not for the reasons Brooks thought.

Oh sure, maybe she'd enjoy one night, a memory for those days when she was president of the PTA with a husband and two point one kids with a house on the Bridle Path or Forest Hill. Which Noah could give her, but Max? Nope. He didn't run in the same financial circles, and even though he had a good nest egg already put aside, and owned his own house, he sure as hell didn't want to play in the same sandbox of Dipwad and his friends. She deserved someone better. Which was the only reason he didn't grab the asshole's finger and break the sucker.

Maybe Hayley sensed his doubts because she placed her hand over Max's and squeezed it. "I trust Max way more than you ever deserved. Now why don't you get back to your date. I'm sure she's not happy about you spending so much time worrying about me instead of her."

A dark-haired guy Hayley had introduced earlier as the bride's brother Nicolas approached. "Hayley, is there a problem? Is Brooks here bothering you?"

"Not at all," Hayley assured Nic. "Darrell was just leaving. Weren't you, Darrell?"

Brooks hesitated, his gaze bouncing between Max and Hayley. Eventually he nodded. As he left, he bumped his shoulder into Max, and muttered, "I'm watching you, Moretti. Hurt her and I'll ruin you."

Despite how much he wanted to change the direction of Dipwad's schnoz from its current north-west orientation to the planet Jupiter, he had to respect that the guy seemed genuinely concerned about Hayley. Then again maybe the guy was a controlling asshole who had mastered the art of manipulating her while presenting a reasonable façade to the rest of the world.

Either way neither of them had any say in Hayley's decisions. If she wanted to date him, or Noah, or anyone other than Dipwad, the choice was all hers.

Hayley squeezed Max's hand and tugged him into his recently-vacated chair. "I'm sorry about that."

"No apologies necessary." He lifted her hand and brushed a kiss across her knuckles. "Why is he even here anyway?"

"He's the groom's second cousin." Nic pulled up a chair and joined them.

Max grunted. "So he's family."

"Yup, and it's hard to uninvite family, even when they're total assholes." Nic eyed Hayley. "Whatever it was he said, forget it. Sophia's furious at him for the way he treated you, and frankly, I'm not impressed either. You're better off without him."

Max decided he liked the guy. They sat and shot the breeze, discussing the upcoming wedding, Nic's hole-in-one in his latest golf tournament that had got him into the playoffs—turned out the guy was a pro golfer, Hayley's upcoming projects and a couple of houses she was contemplating buying before Hayley touched Max's wrist. "Do you want to leave?"

Max debated for a moment, wondering whether to ask her to dance again simply to needle Dipwad who was still eyeing them. Nah, that was something he would have done ten years ago. It wouldn't hurt that their disappearance would bug Dipwad even more because then he'd wonder if Max had taken her back to his place, or stayed the night at hers. Which suited him just fine. "Let's go."

The humidity that accompanied the latest July heat wave blasted them both as they walked from the over-air-conditioned venue. Hayley clung to his arm as they walked across the cobblestones drawing his attention down to the fuck-me heels she'd worn. Damn, he wished she wore a skirt on the job-site every day instead of hiding those fantastic legs beneath her jeans. Because it turned out in addition to being the breast man he'd always thought of himself as, her smooth expanse of thigh and curvy calves were a helluva turn on too. Especially when he imagined them wrapping around his waist.

As they got within sight of his truck, he hit unlock on the key fob. He'd intended to reach past her to open her door, but instead he found himself leaning in, lowering his head until their foreheads nearly touched. The perfume she'd put on earlier had nearly worn off, but the hint of it teased his nostrils, as did the view of a lacy pink bow on her bra.

Her breath hitched and heat poured off her, the air between them crackling. She flattened her hands over his chest, sliding one slim finger through the opening between buttons. "Do you know how often I've fantasized about doing this?"

Oh really? The idea that she might have been picturing him instead of Dipwad sent a blast of pleasure through him. "Yeah?"

"For months." Her tongue made another appearance and her lids fluttered down, hiding her eyes. "How come you've not even kissed me yet?"

It was the *yet* that had Max threading his fingers through her hair to cup the back of her head. The *yet* that had him capturing her lips. Her breath was warm on his cheek as she sighed and sank into the kiss, opening her lips, allowing him entrance. She tasted of merlot and the apple crisp they'd served for dessert, but beneath it was a promise of something more. Of acceptance, of love. A promise that he vowed he would not let slip through his fingers.

Max placed his hands on her hips, and slid one hand beneath her silk shirt touching the bare skin of her midriff. "Did you imagine me touching you like this?"

"Yes." Her answer came out on a sigh as her eyes fluttered closed. "And more."

His touch moved higher beneath her blouse, until he felt the underswell of her breasts. "Have you fantasized about this, *bambina*?" He'd never in his life used that term with a woman, but after hearing Darrell calling her babe, he didn't want to use that generic term. Plus it felt right as it tumbled from his tongue. "Have you been wondering what it would be like when I take off your clothes, and put my mouth on these beauties?"

What color were her nipples, he wondered, though he hoped that he'd soon discover the answer. She'd be responsive too, if the way her breathing kept hitching was an indicator.

"Get your hands off her, Moretti." Something—or someone—yanked on his shirt, pulling him backward. He was slammed into the truck's door, an arm across his throat. "Hayley, are you okay?"

"Of course, I am. Now let him go. Right the fuck now, Darrell."

Darrell released his hold and immediately caught Hayley in his arms. "Look at me, let me see your eyes."

"What the hell?" Hayley shoved him away. "What is your problem, Darrell?"

"I wanted to make sure Moretti hadn't slipped a roofie in your drink."

"What?" Max's jaw dropped. "I don't need to drug my women to get them to kiss me."

Hayley slapped Darrell's chest. "I'm not drugged. Jesus, do you really think that's the only reason I'd be interested in kissing someone? Or was it more that it was because I was kissing someone who wasn't you?"

"The Hayley I knew wouldn't have been caught dead kissing me out in public like this. She would have had more respect. More decorum."

"That's rich coming from the cheater who ended up on the Jumbotron kissing someone who wasn't his girlfriend."

"This is Moretti we're talking about, Hayley. Everyone knows he and that buddy of his share their women. You're destroying your reputation even being seen around him. But if people see you kissing him like that? They're going to think you're a whore. You realize he's probably heard about you wanting to have a threesome and figures you're ripe for the picking."

Shit. He thought they'd kept their threesomes discreet. How the hell had Brooks found out about them? And Hayley wanted one? An already erect Little Max perked up in interest.

"I asked Max out, not the other way around. And neither Max nor Noah have ever been anything but a gentleman around me."

"That's part of their plan. They sweet talk you and make you think they're stand-up guys, but the only reason they're hanging around you is get into your pants. Once they've got you into their bed, they'll move on."

"No, that's your specialty, Dipwad," Max snarled.

Dipwad didn't back off. "Listen, I totally get that you're pissed at me, but when we broke up, you said we were still friends, right? Well, now I'm warning you about him as a friend. Have your fun with Moretti and that other guy if you must. But when you're done, you're going to be looking for a long-term commitment. Marriage, kids, the whole shebang. I'm telling you, babe, you're not going to get it with *him.*"

"Like you were such a catch, Brooks?" Max shot back. It gave him an added layer of satisfaction when Brooks sputtered, waved an arm and walked away. *Score one for Team Moretti.*

Chapter 3

Neither of them spoke as Max pulled a louie in the middle of Parliament Street to get them heading back north. Darrell had departed, but it left Hayley wondering about Max and Noah's reputation. Did they share their girlfriends?

The places Max had touched Hayley still tingled—hell, her whole body was on fire from the simple touch of his fingers on her belly. He'd set her imagination aflame with scenes of her splayed on the bed beneath him, his body a warm blanket, his lips caressing her breasts, his fingers digging into her hips, his cock hard and pulsing inside her. The scene changed to her on her knees in front of him in the shower, sucking him off as warm water caressed her shoulders and trickled down her back.

"You're taking me home?"

"Yeah, unless you want to stop off somewhere else."

While she'd been to his place a couple of times, she'd never had a chance to go beyond the living room and kitchen. She wanted to see his bedroom, to learn if he was neat or messy in private. To snuggle against him in his bed, leave her scent on his pillows. To have her body surrounded by his. "I sort of figured we'd head to your place."

"Normally I'd jump all over that answer, but I don't think that's a good idea right now."

"Because of what Darrell said?"

"Partly." He scrubbed one hand over his mouth. "Look, what Darrell said back there about me not being right for you? He's right. I'm nowhere near in your league. I'm a blue collar worker. I run in totally different circles than your friends."

"Other than Sophia, I look at those people as business associates. I like you, Max. I like Noah too. You're my friends so I don't care if those people approve or don't approve of who I date. It's not going to affect whether one of my houses are going to flip or not. As for blue collar, my family's as blue collar as they get. You know my father works at a pulp and paper mill and my mom has been a secretary, a store clerk and now she's working at a nursing home. You'd fit right in."

"What was he talking to you about before I got back to the table?" Oh. That. "He was trying to explain why he'd cheated on me."

Max snorted. "You mean he admitted he's a total douche."

"No. He tried to say it was my fault."

Actually, he'd said, *"Come on, Hayley, you practically drove me away. You spent all your time at your project houses, and when you weren't working you were slumming with this guy and his buddy. Hell you referred to yourselves as the three musketeers. You're not totally responsible, I cheated on you, I'll own that, but you never wanted to do what I wanted. You were never there for me either."*

Maybe he was right. The first few months they'd been together had been fun, maybe because he'd been from a different world than she'd been used to. But she quickly tired of being on parade all the time. Going out with Darrell meant having to dress up and wear high heels and make up and be aware his friends were appraising how much she'd paid for her dress, whether her rings were real diamonds or cubic zirconia. He'd not been pleased that she'd quit her job and made house flipping her full-time business either, though whether he was unhappy that she'd made more than him the previous year or that he didn't like that she actually did some of the work herself offended him, she wasn't sure. Not that any of it excused that he couldn't keep his dick zipped, but he could have broken it off first. Hell, she should have broken it off before they'd even moved in together.

Shopping at the St. Lawrence Market and wandering the booths at Word on the Street with Noah, or sitting on the beach watching the

Canada Day fireworks beside Max was much more comfortable in jeans and sneakers. Even better they got her sense of humor. And she didn't have to watch everything she said, afraid they'd analyze it to death and then criticize her later. Max and Noah made her feel comfortable where she'd never felt she could be herself even when she was alone with Darrell.

Except now Max was acting weird. Withdrawn, instead of cracking some smart joke.

Damn Darrell. There'd only been three couples playing that night—Sophie and Aiden wouldn't have said anything to anyone, Nic and his girlfriend wouldn't have either. But no, Darrell had to go and open his big mouth and spill her secrets, in front of Max no less. And now the whole ménage issue sat like a fricking Tyrannosaurus Rex between them.

"Noah and I—

"We were playing—"

They spoke together and both immediately stopped.

"You first," Max prompted.

"What Darrell was saying about my sexual fantasy? It was Sophia's birthday party—there were only six of us. We started playing Truth or Dare. Soph dared me to tell us my sexual fantasy and I said I'd always fantasized about having two guys at my beck and call. I guess Darrell took it personally."

"Hey, no judgment from me, okay?"

"Have you and Noah really had threesomes?"

He blew out a breath. "Yes. A couple times, but not recently. I have no idea how Brooks found out about them. I can only assume it's a fairly recent discovery—otherwise he probably would have used the knowledge to try to keep you away from us when you were together. He seems like the insecure type."

He had definitely seemed insecure tonight, hadn't he? Or maybe he always had been but she just hadn't seen it before. "When I first started down this path, Darrell did recommend your competition, and to be honest, I hired them for one house. But I didn't like them—they rushed the work and didn't listen to what I wanted. So I hired your firm for the next job and haven't looked back."

"So we're your second choice then?"

"Sometimes you have to kiss a few frogs to find the prince." She didn't let Max's chuckle stop her. "I didn't know about the threesome, so that's not why I asked you out. Or if it makes a difference to our..." What? Relationship? That made it sound like they were dating. Partnership? Same. "Friendship. I wouldn't judge you for it."

He hmmed. "Good to know. But you notice Noah's not here, and that in the year we've worked together neither of us have ever suggested a threesome."

"I know." Her body softened at the thought of having both of them in her bed, touching her, kissing her...

Once they crossed the Don River, he slanted a glance toward her. "While we're on the subject of Brooks, thank you for sticking up for me but he was right. People judge you for coloring outside the lines—I've seen how they hassle—" He broke off as if he were censoring himself. "Hanging out with us could cause people to question your reputation."

"Who I sleep with won't affect the price of my houses when I sell them. So if anyone wants to judge me because I hang out with you and Noah? That's their damage." She touched his arm as he turned into her driveway. "We've hung out long enough that I know I can trust you." If she was honest with herself, they were practically her best friends. "If I were going to have a threesome with anyone, I'd choose you and Noah."

He shoved the stick into Park and sat back, frowning at the steering wheel. "Sex can change things between friends. Just regular sex can change things, right? But threesomes can be even more of a challenge. They can be absolutely amazing with the right people, but they can also bring out all your insecurities, especially jealousy if you think they're getting more attention than you, or giving too much to the other person. You see a side of them that very few people get to witness."

"See, that's why I think you and Noah would be great. Because you get that it's more than just sex."

He shot her a grin that lit up the entire street. "Sweet cheeks, sex with me is never *just* sex."

Of that she was certain. She stayed silent as he walked her up to her door. She took the leap. "Have you ever discussed having a threesome with me?"

"I'm not going to answer that right now. I want you to think about it. It's not a decision you rush into. What happens if things go wrong, Hayley? If you don't have fun, or you regret it afterwards—you're our client. While business is pretty good with everyone fixing up their houses these days, we don't want to lose your business. And you're also our friend, and even if you never hired us again, I don't want to lose your friendship."

"How long do I have to think about it?"

"As long as you need. No pressure, right?" He brushed a kiss on her cheek and headed back to his car.

"Wait! Aren't you going to come in?"

He faced her, but continued walking backward. "Nope. You have a lot to think about, Ms. O'Connell. And I don't want you to say I used undue influence later."

Chapter 4

He shouldn't have clicked the link. Noah knew it even before his finger touched the iPad's screen, yet he'd done it. In disgust he shoved the tablet away from him. So his father had finally stepped aside and named Sloane, Noah's sister, as President. Not that Sloane would truly have full power—no way would Charles McNaughton allow Sloane, or anyone else, to make a move without his approval. Though Sloane had always had their father's approval. Whereas he...

"Coffee, thank God." Max padded into the kitchen, wearing a pair of board shorts and nothing else. He grabbed a mug and poured himself a cup then settled beside Noah. And picked up the iPad. "Hey, that's Sloane, isn't it?"

"Yup." Max obviously hadn't slept with Hayley—he'd come in far too early, and there'd been no noises of Max making love to Hayley drifting up the stairways. Max could be a noisy lover sometimes. No, for a first date, Max would play the gentleman. He'd take his time and make sure his date felt special, secure, and then when he did stay the night he wasn't the type to sneak out at the crack of dawn leaving them to wake up alone.

"What the fuck?" Max scrolled back, his forehead furrowing. "It says she's the only kid. When you said your father had cut you off, I didn't think you meant he has decided you don't actually *exist*."

Noah shrugged and concentrated on the black nirvana in his mug.

"Did this reporter not do any research? I've a good mind to—"

"Leave it alone, Max. I'm all right with it." Though it stung—okay, more than stung, it was like a katana blade to his guts—his father's reaction wasn't unexpected. "I'm doing what I want to do. I don't need his approval to be happy."

"But he's your father. They're your family."

"Yes, we share the same DNA, but family? No." His friendship with Max had been a source of contention with his father from the first time his father met him at the school.

"I'm not paying for you to go to that school to hang out with a bricklayer's son. You're there to cultivate friendships with people who will help your career. Boys whose fathers you may end up working with when you come work for me." His father had never understood how he longed for his family to be more like Max's. How he wished for dinners that involved laughter and chatter instead of the formal dinners he suffered through. For a mother who fussed over him like Mrs. M. fussed over all her kids as opposed to being ignored by the revolving door of his father's trophy wives.

"It's not right," Max grumbled. "How can they just pretend you don't exist?"

He kept his gaze lowered to hide the emotion flooding him at Max's reaction. Would Max feel the same if he knew Charles McNaughton had threatened to get Max's father fired from his job and blacklisted with the union if Noah continued to stay in contact with Max. It was only that threat that convinced Noah to go to college in BC instead of applying to the University of Toronto. Unfortunately it had taken Noah another four years to realize that was only the first of many demands over his life his father would make. Demands that made him miserable. "It is what it is. No yelling and screaming or getting mad at anyone will change it. As I said, I like where I am. I like what I'm doing. I'm not going to change simply to make him happy."

Never again. Especially if it meant changing his friends to satisfy his father's whims.

"But—"

"Leave it alone, Max. I'm fine with the way things are." He took a deep breath and forced a smile. "Now, tell me how things went last night. I half-expected to find a trail of clothes from the front door to your bedroom. Then I realized you came home alone. Did something go wrong?"

Max contemplated him for a couple seconds before allowing himself to be distracted from the article. "No, it went great. It was... enlightening."

Noah raised his eyebrows. Enlightening wasn't a term Max generally used about a date. Or anything or anyone for that matter. "Oh?"

"Darrell the dipwad was there. He tried to convince Hayley his cheating was all her fault."

Noah snorted. "She didn't buy that load of crap, did she?"

"No, she's too smart for him. But he let slip a certain secret that I found interesting."

"If it's that he has a dick the size of a golf pencil, it's hardly a secret."

Max snorted in amusement. "No argument from this corner, but apparently Miss O'Connell harbors a ménage fantasy."

Huh. Not that it was surprising. Hayley had always impressed him as being confident, and not shy at all. But... "Are you thinking that's why she asked us out? Because she's heard about us sharing women before?"

"Maybe." Max frowned at the iPad and closed the cover, shoving it away. "I know it shouldn't make a difference if she did, but—"

"—But what if she did. You're wanting a long term relationship with her, and you're thinking she's looking at you—us—as a one night stand. She's not. She's said she's not."

Truth be told, Noah liked the idea of having a long-term relationship with her too. If he had his way, it would be a permanent three-way relationship. Not that he'd ever want to pressure Max—or Hayley—into that type of arrangement. While Max claimed his parents were aware of their son's sexual history, they expected their son to settle down sometime in the near future, which meant standing in front of a priest with a bride beside him. Being in a three-way relationship wouldn't stop Hayley from marrying Max, but explaining why another man shared their bed, or if she married him why Max shared their bed, might strain the Moretti's acceptance too far. As progressive as the Morettis were, he was pretty sure they had their limits.

"I left it that it's up to her if she wants to have one with us or not."

"Why do I think there's something you're not telling me?"

"Hayley hasn't cancelled you out for the wedding, right?" Max continued, "so you go with her—you'll fit right in with that crowd, believe me."

"What if she asks me back to her place afterwards?" How awkward would it be if he got to sleep with Hayley when Max had held back.

"Then go with her. Look, I didn't go home with her last night because things got a little weird. The dipwad thought maybe I'd drugged her to get her to go out with me—"

"What the fuck?"

"No, it's okay. It probably worked better that I didn't spend the night with her. This way, she'll have a week to decide if she really wants a threesome, and if she's uncomfortable about it still, she'll let you know one way or another."

"In other words, if she thinks we're perverts—"

"She doesn't think that." Max shook his head. "But it's better to give her space to consider her options right? If she cancels out on your date before Saturday, we both know where we stand, no harm no foul."

Trust Max to have thought everything out. He shoved his coffee mug aside. "So what are the plans for today?"

Max slapped him on the shoulder. "We work our asses off and make her house the best it could be, and show her we're a couple of reliable guys, no matter what rumors Dipwad has been spreading."

AS MUCH AS HAYLEY LOVED Sophia and was happy to be her bridesmaid, sitting at the secondary table sucked. Two of the other bridesmaids and groomsmen were married and were discussing their nanny situation. Another groomsmen sized up the pair of college-aged girls who were playing a drunken game of "fuck, marry, ditch" declaring they would definitely fuck the groomsman eyeing them, marry the groom, but they would ditch the groomsman who hadn't looked up from his phone the entire evening. She'd have much rather have sat next to Noah who was sitting at table at the side chatting with Nic and a couple of his buddies and an older couple—Sophie's aunt and uncle she thought.

She chuckled to herself at the memory of Noah's reaction when he'd first seen her – both coming and going, though she doubted he realized the glass in one of the portraits reflected his pursed lips as he formed a silent whistle at the oh-so-sexy drape of fabric low on her back. She'd loved the warmth of his hand on her back, and the way it would discreetly dip beneath the fabric, as he'd waited with her in the conservatory while the bride and groom and their parents posed and smiled during the endless photo shoot.

Once the speeches and toasts finished and the staff moved in to clear the tables, Hayley bee-lined straight to where Noah stood, a glass of white wine dangling casually from his fingers as if he'd stepped out of a fashion magazine. Even though Noah wasn't one of the wedding party, he'd turned heads with his perfectly tailored grey English-cut suit, complete with a crisply folded white pocket square. Yet as dreamy as he looked, she discovered she preferred him in a T-shirt that didn't hide his pecs or biceps, and a pair of ripped blue jeans that hugged his ass to perfection.

Unfortunately one of the girls who had been playing the FMD game was already there, sizing up Noah as if he were a slab of fresh meat and she was a panther, who was starving to death. Before Hayley could interrupt, Noah shook his head. "Sorry, Ainsley, I'm with someone."

"So ditch her." The girl ran her finger down the buttons on his shirt, batting her eyelashes when she reached his fly. "I'll show you a better time. I was a gymnast in high school. I'm very...flexible."

His scowl deepened. He stepped back, leaving her hand hanging in space. "I'm not interested. And I'm not the type to dump a date."

Ainsley pushed out a hip and rested her hand on it. "It's not like she can't call a cab."

Fuck this. Hayley got in Ainsley's face. "Listen, little girl, you have a lot to learn about poaching on other people's dates."

"Hayley's right." Noah stepped between them. "I came with her, I'll leave with her."

Ainsley huffed but left with a muttered "fucking bitch."

"I've never seen you with your claws out before." Noah's expression made her feel as if she were the only one in the room. "I like it."

"Can't blame her really—she's got good taste." She smoothed her hand over his lapel. "You clean up nice, Mr. McNaughton."

"Right back at you, Ms. O'Connell." He trailed his hands down her arms, letting his gaze wander further, setting her body aflame, "No one here tonight would guess that you handle a sledge hammer like a pro."

"Next time I go out with you, maybe I should bring that sledge hammer with us so I can protect you from the other women who want to ravish you."

His smile dimmed. "They're not interested in me. They're interested in my family's money. While you were having your photo taken earlier, Mrs. Demetrios introduced me to Ainsley and a few of her friends and added *he's Charles McNaughton's son, you know of McNaughton Industries.* They both had a feral glint in their eye, I swear."

"I'm so sorry. I had no idea she'd sic them on you." Or that she would try to sabotage Hayley's chances with him. "I'll protect you from them both then."

He lifted her fingers to his lips. "Thank you. Does that protection extend to protecting me from jealous exes who accuse your dates of drugging you?"

"I couldn't believe he thought that. Max isn't still upset, is he?"

"No. He's not upset."

"Did he also tell you about," she lowered her voice after checking those around her, "the threesome?"

"He did. I know Max told you that we'd be interested in fulfilling your...fantasy, and I'm totally on board, but there's no hurry to make a decision. We'll wait as long as you need. All we need is for you to say the word."

Her breath caught in her throat at the power and sincerity in his answer.

Before she could respond, the DJ came on to announce the first dance between the bride and groom and they turned to watch.

Noah stepped behind her, wrapped his arms around her waist and pulled her against him. This was a man comfortable with public displays of affection. His breath was warm when he leaned in to whisper, "You know Max would say you're wearing that dress backward."

Heads turned as she laughed. "He totally would." She twisted in his arms to wrap her arms around his neck. "I'm so glad I'm with you tonight, Noah. I was afraid this would turn into a real drag."

The air between them crackled with heat. His voice was husky as he replied, "I'm glad I'm here with you too."

When the other couples joined the rest of the wedding party on the dance floor, Noah tilted his head toward the others. "Dance with me?"

Her body reacted when his thigh brushed hers, and again when his hand stroked her spine. Even despite the crowds around them, she wanted Noah to slip his hand lower, to have her whole body skin-to-skin against his.

The music switched to a semi-fast number. She however stayed dancing slow while Noah sped up and she stomped on his foot.

"Sorry," she mumbled. "I wasn't paying attention."

He stopped moving, while he left his arms around her, he tilted his head as if he were trying to see into her thoughts.

"Oh? What are you thinking about?" Though his lips had quirked into a smile, his eyes were serious. "Whether you'll ask me to drive you back to your place? Or mine?"

It would be safer to answer "my place" but the temptation to throw caution aside and be swept away in passion between Noah and Max was overwhelming. *But it could ruin your reputation.* "I was thinking about...Sophia, that's all."

Chicken!

Noah made one of those masculine noises in the back of his throat that she found so sexy. He leaned down to whisper in her ear. "Are you sure you aren't imagining the two of us in bed together? Or maybe the three of us?"

She stepped on his foot again. Thank heavens for the dim lighting that would hide her blush. Someone bumped into her—hard—giving her the perfect excuse to hurry off the dance floor. Noah caught her hand and led her past their table and continued on out of the library. He didn't slow down until they were out of the castle and standing on the balcony overlooking the grounds where yet another wedding reception was taking place in the greenhouse. The evening was hot, the air filled with the scent of fresh cut grass and the masses of flowers filling the gardens.

As much as her body was down with the plan, her head took more convincing. What if they saw a threesome as a one-time event and once the night was finished, she'd never see them again? Or at least as nothing more than a business relationship. She could fall in love with them—either of them—both of them—so easily. While she didn't give a crap what other people thought, she'd met Max's family—his big noisy Italian *Catholic* family—and there was no way either the elder Morettis would look kindly on a woman who slept not only with her son but Noah at the same time. It would probably sour their acceptance of Noah too.

He placed his thumb beneath her chin and lifted it until she looked at him. "No pressure, okay? But we want you to think about it. Max and I both care for you. No one would ever learn about it from us, so your reputation will be safe in our hands. But I won't deny we've talked about sharing you before this. That for the last week, I've gone to bed every night thinking about what it would be like to have you between us in my bed."

Oh hell, now she had that image in her head, she'd never be able to get it out.

"You're thinking about it too, aren't you?" He leaned closer, placing his lips against her ear. "You're thinking about what it would be like to be stretched out on the bed, naked, kissing me while Max goes down on you. You're thinking about what it would be like to alternate between our cocks while you blew us. How it would feel to wake up every morning sandwiched between us. To be the center of our world."

She wanted to be that woman between them. She wanted the heat, the attention, the unrelenting pleasure they'd bring her. Damned straight she was picturing the three of them together.

He cupped her jaw. "We'd treat you right, Hayley. You can trust us."

Her gaze strayed beyond him to where one of the other bridesmaids was hurrying toward her. "Hayley, Sophia's going to throw the bouquet."

He held her in place. "When you're ready, just say the word."

"I'm ready," she whispered. "I want to go back to your place. Tonight."

And then she fled.

HAYLEY SAID YES. OUR place. Tonight.

Max fought a variety of reactions to Noah's text. The first "hell yes!" was quickly followed by "oh shit" and hot on its heels was "you're about to ruin a great friendship." His sensible side, the "take it step-by-step, Moretti" took longer to wedge itself amongst the others and calm down the unexpected jitters currently making his hand shake.

Both he and Noah had talked about Hayley's fantasy—a lot—over the past week. Talked about whether they should do it here at their home, or at hers, or whether to rent a hotel room the way they had before. They'd talked about whether Hayley had sought them out because one of the four people they'd shared a bed with had talked out of turn and what that betrayal might mean.

And they'd talked about how it could destroy their friendship. With Hayley. With each other.

Since it was a long weekend and all the hotels were booked, the location had come down to it being a choice between Hayley's place or theirs. As for their friendship, and his more pressing concern about whether she'd specifically sought them out because someone had told her that they'd had threesomes before, well, he supposed they'd find out by her reaction tomorrow morning.

While he waited for them to return, he paced from the living room to the kitchen wishing he had something to do. They'd spent all of yesterday cleaning the place, attacking dust bunnies on the hardwood and fingerprints on the stainless steel appliances like they were an enemy. He wandered upstairs to his bedroom, swiped a finger along the already-dusted dresser. Straightened the covers on his bed despite them being perfectly flat.

That was another thing they'd had to decide—whose bedroom. Ultimately it had come down to *my house, my rules.* A line he'd never insisted upon with Noah before.

Strange that they'd never argued over any of these details before. Then again, they'd never brought any of their shared partners home before. They'd always rented a hotel suite. He'd told himself it was to protect Noah, but Max now wondered if they'd subconsciously used it to keep a distance between their sexual activities and their home life. Otherwise it could have made things awkward.

He fingered the petals of some daisies Noah had placed on the drafting table he used as a desk. "They're so plain. You should have gotten roses or lilies or something more exotic."

"Haven't you watched when Hayley stages the rooms?" Noah had said. "She always chooses daisies. She says they look happy, like they're smiling and bobbing their heads, so they make the prospective home buyer associate it with happiness."

When he'd asked about the orchids Noah had placed in the bathroom, he'd been told they represented respect and dignity.

Shame was a bitter pill lodged in his throat. He'd been busy ensuring they had plenty of supplies—condoms, a blindfold and fur-lined handcuffs in case she wanted to try a little bondage—thinking about the sex, while Noah considered how to make Hayley comfortable, welcome. Treasured.

Both of them knew they were taking a chance. They had so much to lose if things went badly. Hayley mattered. What she thought of them by the end of the night mattered. His relationship with Noah, both as a business partner and a friend, mattered. Yet not having that night with her, and with Noah, could be something he might always regret.

Stop being so morose, Moretti. You're not the glass half-empty type of guy.

Yes, things could go wrong. But things could go incredibly right too. Tomorrow hadn't happened yet. Tonight, he'd be with Hayley, and Noah too. Tonight would be perfect.

The tightness in his chest eased, he returned to the living room and booted up his favorite video game. "Okay, Drake, let's get ourselves out of this damned submarine."

An hour later, all thoughts of the game were forgotten when Noah parked in the driveway. Noah got out first, and rounded the car to open the passenger side door. Max's view of Hayley was blocked by his roommate, but the moment Noah stepped to the side, Max whistled.

Her dress shimmered with each step she took, so did the earrings that dangled from her ears. Even her hair sparkled—they'd probably put some pins in it or something. When they reached the porch, the door didn't immediately open.

Max peered through the peephole. Noah had stopped and was kissing her. Holy crap, it was sexy. It had nothing to do with how they were both blonde or how they both looked like they'd stepped right out of a fashion magazine. It was the expressions on both of their faces and the way Hayley buried her fingers in Noah's hair. They were lost in each other.

Maybe Hayley had changed her mind. Or maybe Noah had.

Just when the doubt weasels had convinced him Noah's text was a mistake, Noah pulled away and cupped Hayley's face. His voice was muffled, but clear enough for Max to hear him ask Hayley if she still wanted this. That there was no pressure, he could just tell Max it was off.

Hayley's nod, and her verbal reassurance she was sure, had him returning to the living room. Noah would never let him forget it if they found him waiting by the door like an over-anxious schoolboy.

Five minutes passed before the door finally opened and then there she was, standing in his front hall. The beads on her blue dress sparkled, creating an angelic halo. The dark fabric accentuated the creaminess of her skin. And her eyes – he could lose himself in their warmth, just settle right in and bask like his mother's cat in a patch of sunlight. Her lipstick was smudged—and there were traces on Noah's lips. She'd still leave traces of crimson on his dick—and Noah's—by night's end.

Her eyelids lifted to meet his gaze, the long lashes sweeping up to reveal those expressive dark eyes. No hint of fear filled them—lust, yes. Anticipation. Yup, that was there too. She was completely unashamed of what they were about to do.

Hell yes!

Chapter 5

The entire drive over her stomach had flip-flopped as she'd wondered about...everything. The only thing she wasn't questioning was her decision to have the threesome. Being with them both, at the same time, would be amazing—of that she was certain. And that she could trust them. Implicitly. Both for the pleasure they'd give her and their discretion.

Noah had hardly spoken until he pulled in front of a beautifully restored old Victorian two-storey house less than half a block from Lake Ontario. The porch light spilled a soft buttery light over the porch and across the yard, warming the old cedar trim of the house and the red brick sidewalk like a Welcome Home sign. While she knew he did good work and earned every cent he made, to be able to afford a house in The Beach much have cost him over a million dollars, and from the care this one spoke of, probably closer to one point five.

"This is yours?"

"No. It's Max's place—it used to be his grandparents' but when they couldn't look after it anymore, he couldn't bear the thought of strangers living there, someone else cooking in his Nonna's kitchen, so he bought it from them."

He climbed out and rounded the truck to open her door. His hand was warm on the small of her back as he walked her up the front path. Not many guys still had those old fashioned manners which on its own would have made him high on Hayley's list.

He opened the door and stepped aside, allowing her to enter first. Rather than gutting the place for the open concept people loved these days, they'd kept the original footprint of the house. She especially loved the stained glass window at the bottom of the stairs, and the   "Are those the original skirting boards and dado rails? And..oh my God, I love the pine plank flooring, is that original too?"

"They are." Max stood in the middle of a set of French doors. He was wearing a plaid shirt she'd seen him wear a dozen times before, and blue jeans. His feet were bare, which probably explained why she hadn't heard him approach. Or maybe he'd been standing there the whole time. "We'll give you a tour in the morning."

"H-hi. I, uh, decided to take you up on your offer."

"I know."

Before she could ask what happened next, Max lifted her hands and pressed her knuckles to his lips. "*La luna si nascose il suo volto per la vergogna quando sei uscito stasera.*"

Behind her Noah muttered, "What did you do? Spend the night searching the web for romantic Italian sayings?"

Hayley bit back an insane urge to giggle. Max had often complained about how people expected a guy with a name like Moretti to speak fluent Italian, but as a second generation Canadian, he knew a spattering of words but not enough to converse. Which made her suspect that Noah was right. But more, she loved how Noah calling him on it broke the tension that had been gripping her.

When she'd first met them she'd thought their banter was an act just for her, then she'd overheard them when they didn't know she was around, and nope. Max was the joker and Noah his straight man, though Noah had his own droll, self-deprecating humor that most times went right over Max's head.

"Okay, so what does it mean?" Noah asked.

"It's supposed to mean that the moon hid her face in shame when she saw you tonight." Max frowned. "Or it was supposed to, but who knows with these online translators." He shrugged, his face lighting up with his unassuming what-do-I-know grin she'd grown to love. "It was either that or call you *la mia patatina.*"

"What does that mean?"

"My little potato. It's what Max's grandfather calls his grandmother all the time." Like Max, Noah knew a smattering of Italian. Probably because he hung out with the Moretti family as much as Max did.

"He calls her a potato? Why?"

"Because when they're cooked they're soft and tasty." Max shuddered. "I don't want to think about them doin' it like that."

For all his complaining, the warmth in his voice made part of her go squishy inside. For all his tough guy act, Max Moretti had always been a total softie when it came to his family. Over the past two years, she'd met the entire Moretti clan—from him taking them on a tour when he finished a renovation, a Thanksgiving dinner, and an endless number of birthday and anniversary parties—one of the products of such a large family. She'd loved the entire Moretti family's closeness, but that he wasn't shy about showing it? Totally drool worthy.

His voice roughened. "About tonight. If you're having second thoughts, we can still call it off. We won't think any less of you."

The nerves that battered her stomach since she'd walked in settled. When she'd given her sexual fantasy answer at Sophia's party, it had been an off-the-cuff remark, a joke that she'd not expected to ever have fulfilled. Especially with Darrell as a partner. But with Max and Noah as her partners? Her resolve stiffened.

She straightened her shoulders and stepped so she could see them both. "I know what I want. And I want this. Both of you. At the same time. Tonight." Yes, it just felt right. "And of course you have to use condoms."

"We'd insist upon it," Noah answered, his voice deeper and rougher than it had been at the reception. "Good." "It's going to be better than good. It's going to be fantastic." Max lowered his head and caught her lips with his.

Max kissed differently than Noah. More directly. It wasn't a matter of confidence—Noah had plenty of that, but Max was about strength, conviction. He was totally into the kiss, his lips firm. Noah's kisses had been gentle, soft. Questioning, waiting for her to respond. Just...different.

It wasn't that Hayley preferred one over the other. Max was closer to her height, so she didn't feel like she was forcing him to bend over too far. He'd shaved more recently so his skin was softer, though there was something to be said for Noah's light scruff. By the end of the night, they'd both leave marks on her skin. Marks that she'd welcome as badges. Where she'd tasted wine and coffee on Noah, Max was minty from the mouthwash he must have just used. Mouthwash to prepare for her arrival. Since he knew he'd be kissing her. *They'd* be kissing her.

"What?" Max pulled away. "What's wrong?"

"Nothing's wrong." Absolutely nothing. This was her fantasy. Her one shot at them both. The one night she wouldn't have to choose between them, wouldn't have to feel guilty that she'd asked Max out last week and Noah tonight. She caught the hem of his shirt and tugged. "Ditch the shirt, slave boy. I want bare skin against me."

"Your wish is my command." A grin promising he'd soon return the request, Max quickly discarded the shirt and dropped it on the floor. When his hands went to his fly she stopped him.

"No, that's for me to do, slave." She stepped closer again and cupped his jaw between her palms. She kissed him, taking control this time. His erection was a hard pole against her by the time she drew away with a breathy, "I like how you follow orders."

"I liked your orders. But I have a few of my own." He caught her hands and flattened them against his chest. "Noah, undo Hayley's dress, will you? There's a zipper on the right side."

The warmth of Noah's hands and the gentle tug on the zipper had her arching into his touch, but held captive by Max's gaze, she didn't glance over her shoulder to see what Noah was doing. A brush of warm fingers shoved the fabric off her shoulders. She caught it just as it sagged over her breasts. While she might not have any reservations about being naked in front of both of them, there was fricking big window just behind Max—there was no way she'd give the neighbors more of a peep show. "Maybe we should take this upstairs."

Chapter 6

Noah scooped her in his arms and carried her up the stairs knowing Max would follow. Instead of stopping on the second floor and heading to Max's room as they'd agreed, Noah continued to the top floor. To his room. There was nothing stopping them from moving down to Max's room later, but just once he wanted her in his bed. If he stopped at Max's room now, he might never get the chance for her scent to saturate the linen, for her hair to stream over his pillow. Because he was pretty sure by the time this experiment was over, she'd never return to this floor, instead choosing Max over him. If she indeed chose to see either of them again.

After flicking on the light, he slowed his pace and set her on her feet by the end of the bed. She'd been looking around from the moment they'd cleared the stairs, no doubt assessing the décor of his room. Or maybe just checking to make sure it was safe.

He'd known jackshit about decorating before he'd met her—but with each house they'd worked on, Noah had listened to her numerous conversations with her stager about color and lighting, accent walls and accessories, so when it came time to decorate this space, this was all Hayley's design. From the cool grey walls and white wainscoting, and bamboo flooring that reminded him of driftwood, to the subtle lighting in the focal wall that jutted above his king-sized bed. Even the duvet was a copy of one she'd picked out for the house they'd just finished.

Noah collared Hayley's neck with his hand, gratified and relieved when she trusted him enough to lean into his palm. He leaned down to whisper in her ear, "We promise we won't do anything you don't like."

Hayley lifted her face as if seeking him. "I know—I trust you."

He kissed her and once again he tasted a hint of the wine she'd sipped, and the dark chocolate and cherries from the dessert she'd chosen. But where he'd kept his kisses on the porch gentle, now he feasted upon her, teasing and tempting her.

He kissed the curve where her neck met her shoulder then sought Max. A nod had Max slipping her dress over her shoulders. The silky fabric fell to the floor to pool at her feet, leaving her in just a pair of white lacy panties and stiletto high heels.

God, she looked so fucking sexy. He skimmed a hand down her belly, drawing a soft exhalation. They'd already planned that he'd take the lead at first.

Noah's gaze had locked on Hayley's breasts. Hayley had beautiful breasts, bountiful breasts. Breasts he couldn't wait to bury his face—and his cock—in. Which he planned to do later. After he'd thoroughly pleasured Hayley first.

"You're still dressed. Max, ditch the jeans."

"My pleasure." A flip of a button, a wiggle of his hips and Max ditched his jeans, kicking them into a corner.

"Hayley, lean against Max."

Not only would it get her used to the idea of both of them touching her, but it would give him the freedom to take his time going down on her. Man, did he want to taste that sweetness between her thighs.

Max wrapped an arm around Hayley's waist, his skin dark against the porcelain of hers. She twisted her head to look at him—there was an almost visible connection between them that Noah wanted to be part of. Love in Max's eyes, and friendship and trust in Hayley's.

Hayley twisted in Max's arms, draped her arms around his neck, the length of her spine curving like a ballerina's, her breasts pressing against Max's chest, the two of them unaware of anything else, of him. Max caught Hayley's mouth with his... Her soft sigh spoke of need and desire as her eyes fluttered closed. Max cupped her breast, his thumb teasing her nipple that peaked with the attention until she moaned and arched up. Only then did he capture one nipple between his teeth, tugging slightly, earning a sharp intake of breath.

Her eyes still closed, Hayley's head fell back, the pins in her hair sparkling under the overhead lights.

Max was hard angles, muscles covered in tanned skin, made darker from the dark hair, especially over his chest, the cut of muscle sloping over his hips, the heavy erection bobbing from a nest of dark hair at his groin were all angular compared to Hayley's curves, from the plump breasts to the slope from her waist to her hip.

They were a living Vermeer, a study of light and dark, of smooth and hard, of beauty both masculine and feminine.

"You just going to stand there watching, or are you going to join us?" Max asked, using that rough gravelly tone that Noah had only heard when Max was completely turned on.

He turned Hayley so she faced Noah, her mouth slightly swollen, her eyes soft and dark, inviting, making Noah's cock hardened until it was painful.

Noah lowered himself to his knees in front of them, dragging his tongue over her belly.

"Take off her panties. I want her naked," Max ordered.

Her thigh muscles clenched when his fingers touched her hips. Oh, not to hold onto her panties. Oh no. The little minx was so turned on she was squeezing her thighs together to ease the aching burn he knew she was already feeling.

He slipped his thumbs beneath the strings and drew them down over Hayley's thighs, past her knees.

A nudge, and Hayley stepped out of them, her legs spread wide, welcoming, her pussy glistening...

He slipped to his knees to touch the tip of his tongue to her swollen clit. As he'd expected, she bit her lip to try to hide her moan of pleasure. God, he loved how responsive she was. "I'm barely going to have to touch you to make you come, am I, sweet cheeks?"

With a leisurely pace, he licked, tasted and worshipped her, swirling his tongue over her clit. He speared two fingers in her pussy, teasing her, torturing her. A fine sweat beaded on her skin, her legs shook and still he continued. Hayley tangled her fingers in his hair, holding him in place as she ground against him.

Her moans grew wilder, needy, until his cock jerked wanting to take her right the hell now. Except tonight wasn't about him, it was all for her so he held tight to his own needs.

Only when she came apart, crying his name, did Noah sit back on his heels, satisfied.

"Oh, God, that was...amazing," she panted.

Hayley flicked a finger against Noah's tie. "I want you naked too, Noah. It's my fantasy, remember?"

"It is." But it was fast becoming his too.

He shrugged out of his jacket and walked to his closet, aware of them watching him. Piece by piece, he discarded his clothes—drawing out the process of removing his watch and placing it carefully in its velvet lined spot in the top drawer of his dresser. The tie was carefully draped over the same hanger as the jacket, ready to be taken to the cleaners. He opened each button, slowly, aroused that not only was Hayley entranced by his show but he also had Max's undivided attention. A tug on the cufflink on the right sleeve, then the left, he dropped them beside his watch before moving to his shirt.

Their gazes followed him as he turned his back on them and strolled to the hamper, where he discarded the barely-soiled garment. A glance in the mirror showed Max was still watching, though his gaze was glued to Noah's ass, a hunger in it that Noah didn't dare analyze. His heart racing, his body heated and ready, he faced them, a hand casually on his fly. He flicked the button, undid the zipper and let the pants fall to his ankles. His cock ached as Hayley's gaze fell to the bulge in his boxer briefs; his heart hurt when Max switched to watching

Hayley instead. Thumbs hooked in the elastic waist band, he shimmied the briefs over his thighs and stepped out of them.

Hayley caught her bottom lip between her teeth, her gaze sweeping over his chest, his belly, and lingering on his erect cock. His cock jerked when her gaze lingered on his groin as if she'd physically touched him, then it drifted back up his body and rested on his face, her nipples had puckered, her breath had deepened and her eyes were dark pools of passion and need.

He may have imagined Max's latent desire, but Hayley wanted him, as surely as he wanted her.

THEY STOOD THERE, SIDE by side, staring down at her, their faces almost awestruck. She held out her hands, encouraging them to join her. They crawled on the bed, Noah beside her, Max however nudged her knees apart and crawled between her outstretched thighs. Noah played with her breasts, dipping his head over them to suckle, lick and lap. He rasped his teeth over the sensitive buds. When she arched into his mouth, Max toyed with her folds, parting them. He swirled his tongue over her clit...and drove her until she was shaking.

The whole time Noah stroked her back, and kissed her hair, her forehead. He pinched and rolled the sensitive nipples between his fingers. Excitement rippled beneath her skin to every inch of her body, dove deeper in a fiery race to her pussy.

"Stop teasing and fuck me, Max!"

He grinned and reached for the condoms. "All you had to do was ask."

"Forget asking, I'm ordering you."

"Here's an order for you. Get on your belly with your head by Noah's dick."

Unable to stop her smile, she obeyed his instructions and went face to face with Noah's thick veined cock. It might not have been as wide as Max's, but it was at least as long. She curled her fingers and slid them along the shaft.

"Use your mouth, Hayley. Suck him off."

She lowered her head, Noah's musky scent filling her nostrils, and ran her tongue over his bulbous head. A gentle pressure pushed her lower until the shaft filled her mouth. She sucked on it lightly, her tongue teasing the length, earning a groan from Noah.

Behind her, Max positioned his gloved cock at her entrance and eased himself in. "Fuck, you're tight."

"Are you looking for me to swoon and complain about how big you are?" Although in truth, he had one of the biggest cocks she'd seen. Not that she'd seen a lot, but Max was thick and long, and her pussy was being stretched wider than it had been before. And she loved it. But if she said that, it would it make Noah feel inadequate, which he had no reason to, because he put most of the other guys to shame too. The whole bit of having to worry about two male egos was going to be a balancing act.

Hayley's body tightened as yet another orgasm built with each stroke of Max's cock. Yet every time she thought she was almost there, it would slip away. "I keep getting so close and then...it just disappears," she whimpered.

"It's because you're thinking too hard, just close your eyes and feel, Hayley," Noah said quietly.

"Hang on. I've got just the thing." Max bounded off the bed and down the stairs. He returned seconds later with a black silk blindfold in one hand, along with a bottle of lube, and...was that a box of condoms?

"Good thing Mom made me join the boy scouts – I'm always prepared." He placed the lube and the box on the table beside Noah's bed. "When we talked about if you said yes to this, we planned to do this down in my bedroom, so we left all our supplies down there."

"Uh huh." Now she wanted to see exactly what *supplies* they'd stocked. She had a feeling the blindfold was just the beginning. Which sent a very warm glow of anticipation through her.

Max removed a half dozen condoms and dropped them on the table.

"Okay, you're either bragging or really hopeful."

"Hey, don't underestimate a Moretti. Or McNaughton here." He frowned. "Okay, let's try this a little differently. Hayley, have you ever done anal before?"

She nodded.

"Okay, good. Noah, let's trade places. Hayley, I'm going to lie down, and you're going to ride me, okay? And then Noah's going to come in from behind."

There was a shuffling and positioning and she found herself positioned over Max's erect cock. "Okay, Noah, let's blindfold her now."

Noah nodded. "Close your eyes, Hayley."

She lowered her lids, and the cool fabric covered them, cutting off the soft light. It tightened slightly as he fastened it so it wouldn't slip.

"Can you see anything?"

She shook her head. "No."

"Good." The mattress dipped as he climbed back on. "Okay, sit down on Max, and then I'll get you ready for me."

She eased herself over Max's cock. This time he went in much more easily but holy crap she still felt completely stretched. "I'm not sure there's going to be room for you too, Noah."

"It'll hurt a bit at first, but then it's going to blow your mind. You're going to love it, Hayley. Trust us. We're going to make it fantastic for you."

Noah pressed on her shoulders, until she lay flat over Max. Cool fingers trained over her cheeks. "You have the sweetest ass."

"Hey, that makes me self-conscious about mine." Max stuck his lower lip out in a mock pout.

"You've got a great ass too, Moretti. No body shaming here." Noah's hand slid over her ass to between her legs. "Nice firm buttocks. Just how I like 'em."

He swatted Max's hip. "Now stop distracting me or I'll lube you up instead."

Once again he smoothed his hands over her ass, this time stroking a finger along the cleft in the center. "I'm going to add some lube to prepare you, okay?"

"I know."

The finger returned and worked its way in. Another joined it. The whole time Max had his hand between them, playing with her clit. She breathed through the burn as Noah stretched her, forcing herself to concentrate on the pleasure Max was giving her.

Noah closed his hands around her hips, his cock pressed against her, entering her slowly. The two of them murmured reminders to keep breathing, to relax, until Noah was buried deep in her ass.

The sensation of being totally filled in each orifice was overwhelming for a minute, so they stayed in place, not moving. When they finally started moving, all she could do was hang on.

They were right. Not being able to see, made her concentrate only on what she could feel. All she could do was feel. Feel the hair on his thighs rasping the tender inner skin of hers. Feel Max's cock, hard and thick filling her pussy, Noah's cock filling her ass, his balls slapping her clit, each slap reverberating through Max's cock.

It was...liberating. Fascinating. Addictive.

That they had given her this fantasy without belittling or demeaning her meant more than she'd ever be able to express.

Excitement rippled beneath her skin to every inch of her body, dove deeper in a fiery race to her pussy. With each stroke they drove her toward the line her mind had once feared to cross, afraid she'd lose total control. Now it rocketed towards her, stealing her breath, her thoughts.

A moan raked her throat, her entire body tightened and white hot stars dotted the back of her eyes as her climax roared over her, consumed her.

They slowed as she rode out her orgasm, then began their relentless pace again.

Another squeeze and a pull and Hayley's pussy clamped around Max's cock, squeezing, milking him, pulling him deeper until he touched a spot that had her convulsing around him so hard, she screamed with the pleasure.

Her legs shook and lungs ached when she came minutes later for a fourth time, this time taking Max with her. .

With a roar, he lost his rhythm, his cock jerking inside her. Seconds later, Noah swore, his own orgasm warming her ass.

First Hayley, then Noah slumped over Max, their bodies trembling, all three of them panting.

"Holy fuck, that was incredible," Hayley breathed.

"It certainly was."

Max attempted to shift beneath them. "Um, guys, it blew my fucking mind, but I need you to move. I can't breathe."

Noah scrambled back with a muttered, "Sorry." He helped Hayley off of Max. "I'm going to go clean up. I'll be right back."

Soft footsteps padded away from them and there was the sound of running water in the bathroom as gentle hands undid the blindfold and removed it. Max brushed a kiss over her forehead, with a murmured, "You are so beautiful when you come."

She huffed. "Thank you, but personally I think you're full of it. My face feels like it turned bright red and I swear I look like a Halloween mask."

He tapped the end of her nose and stood. "You are beautiful. No arguments."

Max jogged down the stairs, no doubt preferring to use his own bathroom to clean up. Or maybe he had some more toys to try out. If he did, she'd beg for a break before having more sex. She'd lost count of the number of orgasms she'd had, and frankly, she wasn't sure she could have any more.

Noah reappeared and handed her a bottle of water. He waited as she pressed the unopened bottle against her neck to cool herself.

"It works better if you take the cap off and drink it."

She stuck her tongue out at him, but followed his directions and glugged what felt like half the contents. Once she recapped it, he wiped a lingering drop from her bottom lip, then eased her onto her back again. But this time, instead of a tongue or fingers or a cock, he gently pressed a—

She hoisted herself up on her elbows to watch him clean her. "Is that a baby wipe?"

"Yeah, they're handy. And sanitary."

"And best of all," Noah added with a grin over his shoulder as Max returned, "it means less laundry for Max to do."

Max shrugged. "Eh, it's your turn to do the laundry this week."

Hayley giggled. "God, I love you guys."

Chapter 7

Light streaked through a break in the curtains four hours later, but Max still hadn't come up with a solution. His arm was numb since Hayley was resting her head on his shoulder, not that he minded at all. He would have lain there forever, content to act as her personal pillow, except his body insisted it needed attention, and not in the fun way. He slid from the bed and stumbled down to his own bathroom to take care of nature's call before grabbing a quick shower.

When he returned to Noah's bedroom, Hayley had shifted, and was now cuddled with Noah, his leg thrown over her hip, drawing her tight against him. Unwilling to disturb them, Max crept down the stairs. Maybe a plan on how to convince them to stay together permanently would come to him while he was making breakfast.

By the time he returned with the first tray filled with plates of waffles, and all the fixings—a mixture of local strawberries and blueberries, butter, syrup and whipped cream, Hayley's eyes flickered open and unerringly found him.

"Good morning."

It certainly was. God he loved that husky just woken up tone in her voice, and the sleepy heaviness in her eyes.

He whispered, "be right back," and began the long slog down and back up the two flights of stairs, this time carrying a carafe filled with coffee, mugs and cream and sugar (the cream for Hayley—she always asked for extra whenever they were at a restaurant, the sugar for Noah.)

"Next time I'd putting a dumb waiter in," he muttered on the first landing.

Only Noah was in the bed when Max returned, his arms behind his head, and looking extremely satisfied. He tilted his head toward the bathroom. "Listen to her. She's singing."

Max wasn't sure the off-key warbling qualified as singing precisely, but both he and Noah grinned at the upbeat tone.

"We did that," Noah said, almost in awe. "We made her happy."

"We did." And they'd both made Max happy. Life couldn't be any better than this.

"Oooh, coffee! You're the best, Max." Hayley reappeared, lightly brushing a kiss on his cheek before snagging a mug.

She loaded a plate with a selection of the food Max had fixed then clambered onto the bed, and wriggled into place beside Noah. Max pulled up one of the chairs from the reading nook by the window and propped his legs up on the end of the bed.

He marveled at how easy they all were, none of them feeling awkward, or embarrassed. Instead Hayley talked about the wedding, they discussed her plans for the next house, the staging of the one they'd finished.

Hayley waved her fork in the air, the strawberry stabbed on the tines punctuating her words. "You've done amazing things with this place. They're exactly the colors I would have chosen. And the bathroom is divine. If Noah ever moves out, Max, let me know. I know some people who would pay top dollar for a loft like this. It would be better if it had a separate entrance of course."

A shiver racked Max at the thought of Noah moving out. "The original plans called for one but—"

"—I came back and screwed up his plans," Noah added. "But it wouldn't be hard to slap up a couple walls around the stairwell to create a shared vestibule." "

Hay shook her head in confusion. "You came back? Haven't you always lived in Toronto?"

"My father moved us out to BC halfway through grade twelve." Noah regarded his coffee. "I went to college there too. Then about three years ago, Mrs. Moretti sent me a birthday card and since I didn't have any reason to stay in BC anymore, the next thing I knew I'd sublet my apartment and was on a flight back to Toronto."

Max rubbed his chest at the ache in Noah's voice proving that even after all these years, Noah still hurt from his father's rejection.

"Yeah, you should hear the way my nonna tells it." Max raised his voice to a falsetto with a heavy Italian accent, "This boy arrives on the doorstep, with suitcase in hand, and no plans for where he's going to stay, no job prospects."

He pinched his fingers together and waved them in an approximation of his grandmother's broad gesticulations. "You live there with my Maxxie. He needs a good boy like you as a roommate. You take care of each other, help each other like friends do, no?"

Noah snorted. "I'd been here before and knew it needed updating but for some reason I figured they were talking about painting or maybe redoing the hardwood." He hooked his thumb in Max's direction. "Then I walk in and discover hotshot here had torn the walls down to the studs, the water was turned off, and the furnace didn't work—and this was in November, so it was getting pretty chilly at night. I slept on an air mattress in whatever room was in the best shape while Momma's boy slept at his parents' place every night."

Max breathed a sigh of relief that his attempt at humor had lightened Noah's tone. "Hey, you could have slept at my parents', too. That pull-out couch in the basement isn't half bad."

"They had a houseful already without me adding to their burden." With a groan, Noah stood and stretched. "I'm going to grab a shower. You guys want to join me?"

Hayley reached out to trail her fingers over Noah's thighs as he passed. "I'll be there in a minute. I want to finish my waffles."

Max hauled himself to the head of the bed, pounded his fist into one of the pillows, and settled back, his hands clasped behind his head. Which gave him the perfect view of her breasts now that the sheet had fallen to Hayley's lap.

Last night had been...mind blowing. No way did he want today to end and have to let her go. Not so soon. "Tell me you've got more planned for us."

At her hesitation, he lifted himself up on his elbows. "Is something wrong?"

She pushed away the plate and curled one knee beneath her so she faced him. "I want to ask something but I'm worried you'll be insulted."

Oh oh. "I won't be able to tell you if I will be or not unless you ask."

"It's just some guys get twitchy if another guy gets near their *equipment* so to speak, yet last night you and Noah seemed so comfortable with each other's private parts touching."

She'd thought he was comfortable? Okay, maybe later in the night he'd been but when Noah had felt up his ass, he'd cupped balls too—had Hayley been able to see that? Then again since she was on top of him at the time, maybe she'd been able to tell from the way he'd almost jumped through the ceiling.

"First off, that's not a question, that's a statement. But if you're asking if Noah and I are lovers, the answer is no. I mean when we were teens, we did some experimenting one weekend but that's all it was. We've just had threesomes before and it's almost impossible to not have your junk touch." While Max didn't give a duck's fart for what anyone thought, and Noah might freak out if it worried Hayley. Or maybe not. "Does it make a difference to you that we're not concerned about us crossing swords, so to speak? Did it lessen your enjoyment?"

"No." There was no hesitation to her answer. "I just wondered if maybe there was more to your relationship that I realized."

"You're asking if we're gay. If we're a couple."

"I guess. I don't want to end up being a third wheel."

"We're friends," Max assured her. "Best friends. With some weird sexual kinks maybe, but we're not into each other that way." Something flickered across her face. Relief? Or something else he couldn't interpret? "Does that disappoint you?"

Her expression softened into a smile. "No, I guess I just realized I may have some weird sexual kinks too and I'm finding it disconcerting to admit that to myself."

She tilted her head, listening. "Sounds like Noah's in the shower." A wicked grinned lit up her face. "I think I'm going to run up and join him, offer to soap him up. Want to join me?"

"Of course."

As he trailed her up the stairs, his dick already hardening at the idea of being inside her again, Max realized he was in trouble. Though he'd never admitted it to Noah, Max had fallen hella deep in love with Hayley. The get-down-on-one-knee-and-pledge-himself-for-life type of love. And tied to that issue, or maybe it was an issue all its own, he was pretty sure Noah was in love with Hayley too.

"You promised you'd fulfill her fantasy, dude," he muttered to himself. But now they'd fulfilled her fantasy, would she not see either of them as a permanent relationship prospect but as a one and done?

Chapter 8

It wasn't the warmth of the shower that had Noah leaning his cheek against the cool quartz wall. He'd settled onto the bench out of the water's reach, sure that the bones in his legs had changed to rubber. Being with Hayley—at the wedding reception, dancing with her, chatting on the way home, had been his personal fantasy. She'd been funny and open, supportive. And looked only at him without the "his family has money" glint in her eye. Being inside her had been holy-shit-I-don't-want-this-to-end. Ever.

She was the type of woman that could reach into his soul. She'd hung around enough rich people to realize money didn't buy happiness. That rich families could be just as fucked up as poor. In fact, maybe more because people like his father surrounded themselves with yes men. People who would never say boo if they were way out of line. Max's family kept him level-headed. They weren't afraid to slap the side of his head—literally—when he screwed up. And when things went wrong, they were there for each other.

Noah banged his head against the marble, welcoming the ache it caused. Why the hell had he agreed to share her tonight? Why hadn't he taken her back to her place after the wedding and made love to her by himself, then arranged for the threesome some other time?

Because Max hadn't brought her home the week before. Instead he'd given her space to think about having the threesome, but also time to decide if she wanted to date either of them. For Noah to take advantage of Max's chivalry, well, that wouldn't make him a good friend. To either of them. Except if Hayley had seen Max's face just now, which he was pretty sure she had, Noah was certain they might as well hang a runner-up ribbon in the "who does Hayley want" competition.

Which hurt like a splinter under his fingernail. Hell, under all ten fingernails. Toenails too.

"Noah? Mind if we join you?" Hayley's voice floated out of the bedroom, the warmth in her voice descending around his shoulders, soothing his psyche, like a comforting blanket. "I've just decided soaping both you guys up in a shower is part of my fantasy."

"And we're here to fulfill her fantasy, aren't we, Noah?" There was a weird tone in Max's voice, not playful but almost as if he were trying to warn Noah of something. Why would Max think he'd object? If Hayley's fantasy included a shower scene, they'd already agreed they'd do anything to make her happy.

Except it wasn't just Hayley whose fantasies were being fulfilled, was it? The heat in Max's face just now had brought back every memory, every need and desire, of that long weekend in May back in high school. Hearing the tenderness in his voice, and how it changed to rough grunts, feeling the slide of his cock against Noah's through the warm barrier Hayley provided combined with the heat and longing, pure sex in his eyes when he came...

His cock jerked at the memory. Shit. *You've let yourself fall in love with her, doofus.* He was pretty damned sure Max was in love with her too and now they'd be in competition with each other. He banged his head once more. "What the fuck were you thinking agreeing to this threesome, McNaughton? You've destroyed two friendships now."

"Noah?" The door creaked open and Max peered around it. His gaze zeroed in on his erection and he grinned. "Oh good, you're not on the can."

Without waiting for Noah to respond, he walked in, Hayley trailing him.

"Is your bathroom like this, Max? I'd love to see it." Hayley traced her fingers over the stone.

Jesus, McNaughton, when did you become so insecure?

When he realized it was a competition between him and his best friend for the woman who could be *the one*.

"You guys did a fantastic job with this space." Her smile lit up the room. *Geez, you are totally insecure if her liking your choice of tile makes you feel better.* "And it's huge!"

"Yup, there's room enough for six people." He moved aside letting Hayley step under the spray. The water beaded and sluiced down her, dripping off her nipples in an erotic waterfall. His semi hardened into a full-on woody.

"He's not exaggerating." Max casually slid out of his clothes and eased into the shower stall. "My entire family dropped by when we were laying out the wall lines. The entire herd fit into this area which totally scandalized Mom."

"Yeah, but your father approved." After his wife and daughters had wandered back into the bedroom, Mr. Moretti had murmured something about it being big enough to have an orgy. And then he'd winked. God, he loved that old man.

Hayley picked up the fresh bar of soap Noah had placed there as an afterthought. It was a special French milled soap that had been a client's thank you gift, but up until now the floral scent had kept him from using it. "Hmm, pretty."

"Just remind me to shower with my own soap before I go out again," Max grumbled. He dropped the soap and cursed, bent to pick it up and dropped it again.

Noah bent to retrieve the bar as it skidded across his foot and held it out to Max. Who jumped back like he'd been bitten. "Seriously? It's not like you've not been in a shower with me before? Or have you forgotten high school, where we showered with like twenty other guys?"

And had a few threesomes before but he was reluctant to remind Hayley of that fact.

"Well, I haven't had the pleasure of showering with you both before, and I intend to take full advantage of it" Her hands coated in suds, Hayley splayed her hands over Noah's chest, slid them over his belly and circled her fingers around his cock, stroking it lightly.

"Fuck that feels good." He closed his eyes, struggling not to come in her hand like a damned teenager. She adjusted her hold, the stroking gaining more strength.

Noah couldn't stop the groan that escaped his throat. How many nights since he'd met Hayley had he imaged himself in this exact scenario? How many nights had that fantasy ended up with him jerking off?

While Noah was just getting into the kiss, preparing to take it deeper, ready to turn Hayley to the wall and hitch up one leg and enter her, he glanced up and noticed Max's eyes locked not on Hayley but on him.

Watching.

Judging?

He ended the kiss, gently setting Hayley back a step and met Max's gaze head on. "Do we have a problem?"

Max heaved a shuddered breath. "No. No problem. We said we'd do anything Hayley wanted this weekend. And I'm still all in for that."

For all his assurances, Max left the stall, snatched a towel, wrapped it around his hips, then wheeled to nail Noah with a glare that could have broken the marble "I need a coffee."

Noah dragged a breath into burning lungs. It was Hayley who had initiated the kiss, and given the ache in his balls from not finishing within her, there was no denying how much he'd enjoyed it. Hayley's nipples were hard against his chest, her moans were of passion not complaint. You didn't do anything wrong. Max had never gotten jealous like this before.

He's freaking out because it's Hayley I'm kissing. Had Max guessed this was more than just sex to Noah? Were they about to find themselves in a fight for her attention?

He really had to get down there, find Max, talk to him, tell him that enjoying a mutual kiss didn't mean Max's world was ending. And hope that Max would listen. Except what would he say? Because he sure as hell wasn't going to back off. Something between them—Hayley and him, Hayley and Max—had changed this weekend. And Noah wasn't prepared to back away from Hayley anymore than Max was.

Holy fuck. He loved her. If he was honest with himself, he'd loved her for a long time now.

Except Max loved her too.

Feeling like the stability of his world was crumbling beneath him, Noah stumbled out of the shower stall, seeking somewhere to hide, except the damned bathroom had fucking mirrors everywhere. Everywhere he looked, Hayley was watching him, her expression worried. God, she was everything he'd dreamed of waking up to in the morning.

"I need to talk to Max. Figure out what's going on in his head." Figure out what was going on in his own head. His own heart.

Hayley shivered, though whether from emotion or because the previously humid air was cooling, Noah wasn't sure. "Has this ever happened before?"

What? Max rushing out? Max being jealous? Both men falling in love with the same woman? Unable to speak he shook his head.

"I've jumbled everything up, haven't I?"

He cupped her jaw in his palm. "Whatever is going on with him" between us "is not on you."

He lifted the robe hanging on the back of the door and wrapped it around her, then snagged a towel from the shelf and used it to dry her hair. Once he'd lead her out of the shower, he grabbed another towel and wrapped it around his hips while trying to ignore the fear screaming that he'd lost Max's trust. And his friendship.

"I'd never do anything to hurt either of you,." she continued, her voice softening, "Please, Noah, you have to believe me."

He blew out a breath. "I do." He ran his hand through his hair. He swallowed, harder to do over the lump forming in his throat. "I need to talk to him." Pound some sense into his head?

What sense? That Hayley would be better suited with him over Max? Because he wasn't sure that was true. Max had a huge loving family who would welcome Hayley with open arms, and while Noah could support himself, and her, she didn't need monetary support. She needed...family. Something he couldn't give her.

Her shoulders slumped. "I guess this weekend wasn't such a great idea."

"I don't regret a second." He feathered his fingers through her hair so she couldn't hide behind it. "I sure as hell have enjoyed being with you."

"I've enjoyed it too." She sniffed, her eyes glistening with unshed tears.

"No one here did anything wrong. You do not have to apologize for anything."

"Then why do I feel like...this? Like I've damaged your friendship?"

"Not your fault." The truth is I've been half in love with you since I met you. Max has been too. Either one of us would love to continue dating you. Marrying you. I'm pretty sure Max has been imagining your kids already. But he couldn't dump that on her right now. "I don't want you to think we used you for our own amusement last night or this morning. Our main goal was making sure you were satisfied. That you enjoyed yourself and lived out your fantasy."

"Thank you."

"I need to go check on Max. Will you still be here once we've got things straightened out?"

"Of course. I'll wait as long as you need me to." The warmth of her hand on his chest eased him. "I need to dry my hair before it ends up all tangled."

He pressed a kiss to her forehead, wishing she'd stay forever, but at this stage, he couldn't figure out how that would be possible.

Chapter 9

Leaving Hayley in the bathroom, Noah walked into the bedroom, hoping to find Max, only to find it empty. The bed was still rumpled, the pillow on the right side still contained the dent of Hayley's head. His hand hovered over it, wanting to pick it up, inhale her scent, memorize it. Instead he backed away. How his world, that had been so joyful this morning, suddenly tilted on its axis and dumped him on his ass so quickly?

He snagged a pair of jeans and a worn UBC t-shirt from his dresser and ran down to Max's bedroom, only to find it empty too. *Shit, he'd run.* A clank of metal drifted upstairs. Max was in the kitchen. Thank God, he still had a chance.

Max was loading the dishwasher when Noah arrived in the kitchen. Like Noah he was wearing a pair of jeans, but Max hadn't bothered with a shirt.

Maybe he made a sound because Max straightened quickly and faced Noah, though he never looked directly at Noah, instead staring past him for a second before it zipped to the fridge, to the floor, then settled on the microwave.

"What's going on? Why'd you run out like that? Hayley thinks you're mad at her, that she's done something wrong." Okay, that wasn't exactly what she'd said but he'd read the subtext.

"Fuck you. I needed coffee, that's all."

Fuck, don't do this, Max. Don't shrug off what we both know you felt. "Coffee, huh?"

"Yeah. Don't pretend there was more to it than there was. You know I'm not a morning person without my coffee."

"I know, but—"

"—but we'd promised we'd fulfill Hayley's fantasy. Yeah, I got it. I...I just couldn't take watching Hayley with her hand around your dick, watching her jerk you off, okay?"

"You're jealous."

"No." The answer came too quickly. Max looked away. "Maybe."

Max returned to loading the dishwasher, restacking dishes he'd already loaded, his movements careful, precise. A sign he was hanging on by a thread. "Has Hayley left?"

"She's still upstairs doing her hair."

"Good." He moved two bread and butter plates from the bottom rack to the top.

"Max, we need to talk about this."

"I told you, there's nothing to talk about." The two bowls that had held the strawberries and blueberries were carefully nestled where the bread plates had been, the three plates still sticky with syrup were added, then moved one rung over, and over again. "I'll drive Hayley home when she comes down."

"We'll see what she wants." It would probably be better for Hayley to take a cab home rather than be subjected to the drama playing out here. Besides, he was afraid that if Max got behind the wheel, he'd either wrap the vehicle around a hydro pole or get on the 401 and never be seen again.

When Max removed the filled cutlery rack and started reorganizing the knives along the back, the forks in the middle, the spoons in the front, where normally he shoved them in randomly, Noah had had enough. He grabbed the plastic rack and tossed it in the sink. "Damn it, Max, stop this. Talk to me. Stop trying to pretend nothing's happened."

"I told you, I'm fine. I don't need to talk."

Fuck this. "How about *I* talk, and you listen then, huh?"

Max stalked to the sink and retrieved the basket. "You're gonna talk anyway. So say it and then leave me the fuck alone."

Noah drummed his fingers on the counter. What tack should he take? "I think after last night, after having the best sex in our lives—and you can't deny it was fucking great last night, you realized you're love with Hayley and don't want to share her."

Max wasn't looking at him, but Noah could tell from the way his hands stilled over the cutlery that he was listening.

"I think being with Hayley meant more to you than our usual games. I think you were jealous of me up there and you can't deal."

Max finally faced him, resting his hips against the counter, and folded his arms across his chest. "You know what I think? *I* think you're projecting. That you're in love with Hayley and that you don't want to share her with me."

Noah forced himself to stand there, as if Max's statement might not be absolutely true.

"You're right. I do love Hayley. But I wasn't jealous of you being with her. I wasn't the one who stomped out of the bathroom just now."

"You didn't stomp out because it was your cock her hand was wrapped around. You won. I get it."

"Max," Noah said, keeping a careful control of his tone. "I love Hayley. But I value our friendship too. And right now you're acting like a fucking dickhead."

"Oh for fuck's sake."

"You're jealous. You just admitted it. You can't stand sharing Hayley. You're threatened by me even being near her"

"I'm the one who told you about Hayley's fantasy, I'm the one who suggested the threesome. I wouldn't have mentioned it, or invited you, if I was threatened by you."

"And yet here we are," Noah said quietly. "Both admitting we love her." And again, I wasn't the one who stomped out of the bathroom like a three-year-old having a temper tantrum at having to share his toys.

"Yeah. I love her."

"I know."

"Do you love her enough that you'll step away if I tell you to?"

"That's not your choice. It's Hayley's." How the hell had they ended up here? Was it going to affect their business partnership too?

"You figure she's going to choose you because you're richer than I am, don't you? Because you can give her a life like Dipwad could have without all the strings attached."

"You can give her something I never could."

"What's that?"

"Your family."

Max blinked, regrouped then stabbed his fingers through his hair, setting it standing up on end. "You don't know she wouldn't choose you over me."

"You're right. I don't. I don't know if she'd choose either of us." Noah dropped his hands to his side and shrugged. "But as fun as the threesome was, this weekend, this fantasy, is over. Done. If she is forced to choose, she'll want you. A good man with a stable well-paying job, a supportive family, who can afford a nice house in a good area and who will support her career. Yeah, you're pure gold, Moretti."

Shit. And there it was. The real truth. The one he'd been denying all these years.

"Whereas me?" Noah continued, "I'll always be that awkward pity invitation you set an extra chair out for at Thanksgiving and Christmas dinners because you feel sorry that I don't have any family. If you and Hayley have kids, you'll have them call me Uncle Noah, but won't have an explanation for why I keep hanging around."

Aw fuck, he did have to leave.

"Anyway, I'm going to find somewhere to live and get out of your hair." Ottawa, maybe. Or Montreal. Claim a table at one of the restaurants on Crescent Street, and watch the world go by. "I'll have my lawyer contact yours to dissolve M&M equally and you can find a new carpenter to work with."

Max choked. "Wait. I didn't say you had to move out. And now you're talking about dissolving the company? What the fuck?"

Chapter 10

Jesus, what the fuck had just happened? Not only might he lose Hayley but he might lose Noah too? While Noah patiently leaned against the counter watching him, Max paced around the kitchen island.

Yesterday he knew exactly who he was, what he wanted. Yesterday he knew Noah was more than just his business partner, he knew Noah was his best friend, that Noah was like a brother from a different mother.

Then he'd seen the love for Hayley in Noah's eyes, and he'd panicked.

Because he'd realized they both wanted the same woman.

He stole a glance at Noah who was watching him, his expression guarded. "So what do we do now?"

"There's only one thing to do, bro. Bring Hayley down here and discuss the situation."

"Make her choose? Right here, right now?"

Shit. "You're saying we're going to stand in front of her and tell her why she should choose? Sell ourselves like we're a freaking product on Shark Tank? She'll run as fast as she can in the other direction."

Noah's gaze finally dropped momentarily. "Yeah, you're right. We're not thinking this through, are we?"

"I'd say you're thinking with your balls, not your brains," Hayley said from the hallway door.

MAX JUMPED TO HIS FEET, his mouth flapping, his eyes darting between her and Noah. "H-how-how long have you been standing there?"

Should she admit she'd crept down the stairs when she'd heard her name? That she'd stood here in the doorway listening as they discussed making her choose between them?

What the hell had she done? Had they done? "Long enough to hear I've come between you two and realize the testosterone level seems to be a little thick in here."

"

Noah swore under his breath. "It's not your fault if you're blaming yourself."

He was right there. They'd promised they did this all the time, that it would be a one night deal and then they'd move on and now they were wanting a permanent relationship with her?

It didn't matter who she chose, their friendship would shatter. Their business too. She couldn't live with herself no matter which choice she made.

"I won't make a decision between you. I won't do that to either of you. So don't even think of making me choose Team Max or Team Noah. It won't work."

"Okay," Noah said, his voice quiet. He slanted a glance toward Max before meeting her gaze once more. "But I think Max and I can both agree, we are definitely both Team Hayley."

"Don't do this to me. Don't put me in the middle." Her voice, her heart, fractured as she spoke.

"There is another alternative," Max said slowly. "One where you don't have to choose."

"What's that?"

"You don't choose. We live together, all three of us." Max frowned at Noah. "Could you do that? Without getting jealous?"

Noah's eyebrows had arched near his hairline. "Right back you, Moretti. You're the asshole who stormed out of the bathroom ten minutes ago like a fucking jealous teenager."

"Yeah, and that's on me."

"You're an amazing woman, Hayley," Noah said quietly. "We need to show you that it's possible for us to love you without either of us being jealous. Stay with us one more day. Let us show you how much we love you."

Noah held out a hand to her, and she walked as if there were some magnet drawing her to him, a force she couldn't resist. Which she wouldn't have anyway. Damn he was good. "You should be writing Hallmark cards."

"You are so beautiful, Hayley." He cupped her face between his palms and claimed her mouth.

Unable to resist, she skimmed her palms up Noah's bare chest, his skin warm and smooth, and beneath the skin, his muscles tight and firm. With a groaned, "Hayley," he tightened his hold, pressing his erection hard against her belly.

She glanced at Max. Max whose face was filled with a mixture of love and lust. Was he hiding that jealousy Noah had accused him of? Or was he finding a way to deal with it? And how the hell was she going to choose between them?

As if sensing her doubts, Max stepped behind her, his hands resting firmly on her shoulders grounding her, his body warm and strong, a balance to her whirling emotions. She let her head fall back on his shoulder, closed her eyes, as he dragged his lips down her neck, over her shoulders. His hips pressed his rigid cock against her ass, a promise of what was to come.

Between them, they made her feel more than wanted. More than lusted after. She wanted this. She wanted them.

With them, she felt...needed.

Cherished.

Chapter 11

She didn't hear them discuss it, but somehow the two men moved in unison, Noah taking her left hand, Max her right, leading her to the stairwell off of the kitchen. This one stopped at the second floor.

Sunlight streamed through an original stained glass window that overlooked the back yard and down the hallway, gleaming off the streaky bamboo floor. She only got a glimpse of blue walls and pine furniture before both men sandwiched her between them, lifting the UBC shirt she'd borrowed from Noah's wardrobe over her head.

"Mmm," Noah murmured. "I'm never going to be able to wear that shirt again without getting a hard-on."

Two sets of hands skimmed her body, front and back. Noah cupped her breasts in his palms, and bent his head to lash them with his tongue while Max slowed his hands over the curve of her ass. "Noah's right. You have the sweetest ass."

"Sweet and tight and hot," Noah agreed around her nipple. "Just like her pussy."

Max's hand slipped between her legs and unerringly found her clit, teasing it. Between his attention to her clit and Noah's teasing of her nipples, Hayley's knees wobbled so hard she dug her fingers into Noah's shoulders to stay upright.

"Let's get her on the bed, Max." Noah walked her backward until her knees hit the mattress and she toppled onto it.

Max appeared beside him, a hungry and satisfied look in his eyes. "Do you know how many times I've fantasized about having you in my bed?"

She shook her head. His lids drooped and he crawled onto the bed, over her, his cock a hard rod pressing into her belly. "Every night since I've met you."

He lowered his head and caught her mouth with his with a hunger that couldn't be satiated. Last night he'd been gentle, as if he was afraid she might break. Today he was rougher, demanding, and she loved every minute of it. Her lips were swollen by the time he finally pulled away, sweat making their skin slide wherever they touched. He touched his thumb to her bottom lip, slid it from one side to another, his touch feather-light compared to his kiss. "I love you, Hayley. Don't ever doubt it."

"I love you too," she whispered. She hadn't intended to say those words yet she couldn't deny what she felt. She loved him. She loved them both.

The mattress dipped as Noah knelt beside them, his gaze locked on her mouth.

Her pulse racing, Hayley leaned up, capturing Noah's head and bringing it down to her mouth. He plundered her mouth with a desperation he'd not had before, devouring her. Max watched them, his eyes dark not with anger or jealousy as she was afraid but with lust and love.

She raised her other arm and tugged Max down to join them.

Hayley's body reacted at the touches they shared, the way they explored her body, kisses pressed hastily on her shoulder, lingering over her neck, sighs when a particularly sensitive spot roused her deep within. Veins on their arms strained as they clutched each other.

His eyes meeting Hayley's, as if willing her to watch, Noah wrapped his hand around his cock, gripping it with a force she never would have dared, a bead glistening at its straining head.

Noah blew out a long slow breath and squeezed his cock at the base. "Fuck, that was close."

Once he regained control, he gestured to the spot between him and Max. "Hayley, come on up here, baby."

Hayley settled into the spot he'd just vacated as Noah rustled in one of the bedside table drawers. Straightening, he handed a foil-clad condom to Hayley, and tossed another at the foot of the bed along with a bottle of lube.

"We're going to take it slow, okay? I promise, I'm going to make it so good for you, Hayley. Do you trust me?"

Hayley nodded. "Yeah. I do."

Noah looked at Hayley, Max following his gaze. "And you'll make it good for Hayley too, won't you, Max? Because she's the whole reason we're here. We have to show her how much she means to us. That she's the center of our world. Can you do that, Max?"

"Of course." He said it so reverently Hayley had to look away to hide the emotion swamping her.

"Good. Stay right there."

Her gaze followed Noah as he stretched to the bedside table and grabbed the lube, his back muscles rippling with strength, his glutes bunching and stretching with each movement.

NOAH WASN'T GOING TO fucking survive the way today was going. He'd gone from happy and content while they were eating breakfast, to shocked and confused at Max's jealousy, to worried that he'd lost both Max and Hayley, and may have even lost the business he and Max had created.

If Hayley accepted the idea he was about to suggest, that they make this threesome a permanent arrangement, he would float to the ceiling. The idea that he'd actually have the support, the love, the family he craved had been the stuff of dreams. No, he'd never dared dream such a solution.

But for now, he had Hayley with him, in his bed, even if he had to share her with Max, he'd do it willingly, happily, if it kept Hayley returning to him tomorrow, and every day after that. No. Don't think that far ahead.

Today is the first day of the rest of your life, carpe diem, and all that crap. Today was a day he was fucking *never* going to forget.

He handed Max the lube then frowned. Shit, they'd forgotten to grab a towel. He swung off the bed and headed to the bathroom. "Don't move."

"You've got a great ass, you know that, McNaughton?" Hayley called.

Keep it light.

"It's from climbing all the fricking ladders Max is too afraid to climb," Noah grabbed a towel off the shelf, flung the towel over his shoulder, and returned to the bedroom, not at all ashamed of his cock proud and heavy bouncing off his belly.

Holy fuck, Hayley's gaze was still locked on him, a hunger in her expression. She licked her bottom lip. He was pretty sure it wasn't a deliberate come but holy fuck it made him hard, especially as his cock remembered how she'd sucked him off the night before, knew the pleasure her mouth gave him.

His gaze settled on the thin line of pointing to Hayley's glistening folds. *Mine.* Mine and Max's, he amended. Noah changed his focus to seek Max's face, and found an expression of awe, and lust, and maybe a touch of fear too.

"We're going to do this almost the same as we did last night. Just in reverse. Hayley, you're going to ride me and Max'll be buried in your lovely tight ass."

Hayley straddled him, lowering herself onto his rock-hard dick. Her hair was tangled around her shoulders, her lips were swollen from their kisses, her breasts still bore evidence of stubble-burn though whether from last night or this morning, he wasn't sure. But she'd never looked more beautiful to him.

Mine.

Fuck, it took every ounce of control not to grab her hips and pump into her.

"Noah? Are you all right?"

None of this would have happened if she hadn't set the wheels of this amazing journey in motion.

Mine and Max's.

He banded an arm around her waist and drew her against him, kissing her, nibbling at her neck, sucking hard enough that it would leave a mark. A proclamation of *she is ours* for the world to see.

He squeezed her behind and growled, "Climb up on the bed, Max. Get her ready."

Max grinned and quickly obeyed. Their mutual groans as he slowly pushed himself into Hayley's ass had Noah's balls tightening painfully with each inch Max's cock disappeared into her glistening cleft.

Apparently he wasn't the only one having trouble at control. "Oh fuck." Max clenched his eyes shut and muttered, "Oh fuck, I'm going to come."

Strangely the stoppage of movement caused a severe ache in Noah's balls.

"Move, damn it, Max. fuck it all to hell, move. You're in charge now. You set the pace."

It was awkward at first, as he and Max coordinated their rhythm, but finally they found their grove.

If they did this again, he'd flip Hayley face up and have her hook her legs over Max's shoulders. He played with her breasts, loving the hitch of her breath as he played with her nipples, feeling her rhythmically tighten around him to Max's thrusts. It was all he could do to just hang on and ride it out.

"Max, Noah, someone touch me," Hayley begged. Max twisted slightly as he slipped a hand between them.

He could tell the moment Max reached Hayley's clit, as Hayley's body clamped down around his shaft. Noah clenched his hands in the bed covers in a desperate attempt to hold on and not buck beneath her which would mess up their rhythm.

Max's eyes lost focus, practically rolled back in his head, before they scrunched closed, his head kicking back, his chest arching up. "Fuck. She's coming. Oh fuck, it's too much, too much...Oh *fuck, holy fuck, yes*.".

Noah couldn't hold off. He dug his fingers into covers even tighter and held on for the ride, each jerk of Hayley's hips milking him until he was drained.

His body trembling, and his mind whirling, Noah's breath hitched as Hayley slipped off him and rolled onto the bed beside him. Max stared up at them both, his eyes dark, his expression filled with wonder, and, maybe a little confusion. "Holy fucking shit. Do you think this could work? Like if we did this permanently?"

"I think it could." He hadn't felt jealous at all and if he was reading Max's reaction correctly the other man hadn't either.

He sought Hayley's mouth next. It was her touch, her lips on his, her fingers curling in his hair, her palm flattened on his chest, that settled him, that proved it wasn't a dream. He might have started this weekend thinking he was fulfilling her fantasy but she and Max had just fulfilled his.

Chapter 12

Hayley awoke clinging to one side of the unfamiliar bed, something heavy on one leg and some deep rhythmic sound. She cracked open an eye and peered at the offending trespasser to discover Max's head resting on her thigh, the rest of him sprawled diagonally across the mattress, snoring.

His face was relaxed, looking younger than she'd ever seen him before.

She glanced around, looking for Noah, realizing the sun had moved, no longer casting bright streamers through the room.

Noah sat in a blue wingchair by the window, his legs stretched out and crossed at the ankle, his hair tousled, and completely, confidently naked. And supremely pleased with himself. "Hey there, sleepy head."

She scrubbed her hands over her face and twisted in an effort to find an alarm clock, but couldn't. Right. At some point they'd moved from Noah's bedroom to Max's. Was that yesterday? Or this morning? "What time is it?"

"Nearly four o'clock. In the afternoon."

She inched out from under Max and dashed to the bathroom to quickly take care of Mother Nature's demands. It wasn't until she returned to the bedroom that she noticed the giant white maple leaf painted over the bed. And the Maple Leaf memorabilia, including a Gilmour jersey, holding a place of pride in a replica locker. Even the ceiling light was a replica of the Maple Leaf scoreboard. "Wow. Talk about a—" teenaged boy's room "—real man cave."

Noah chuckled, though there was softness in his eyes. "You know Max. He's always been a sucker for the underdog."

"Hey, true fans stick by their team, no matter what," Max mumbled from the bed. "Their time will come."

Hayley poked him in the belly. "You just hope it'll be in your lifetime."

"Says the Ottawa Senators loving traitor." Or at least she thought that was what Max said, but he'd buried his head under the pillow and his speech was now muffled.

Hayley wandered over to the drafting table in the corner. She stroked the petals of the daisies, smiling at the blooms as they bobbed and nodded at her touch.

"Noah bought them for you." Max had rolled onto his side and was watching her, his expression wary. "I, uh, hadn't even thought of flowers. I was more worried about...well, condoms and stuff."

"I like the flowers, they're pretty" she said gently, "but they aren't as important as the condoms."

"But you deserve pretty."

A phone rang—the Hockey Night in Canada theme familiar to every Canadian. Noah picked it up from the night table beside him and held it up for Max to see. "It's your mom."

"Shit, I've got to take it or she'll come over to see why I'm not picking up." He jumped from the bed, grabbed the phone and raced into the hallway, his voice fading as he trod down the stairs. "Hey, Ma, what's doin'?"

Hayley settled back on the bed, pulling her legs beneath her. "Do you think we could really make it work? The three of us?"

"I think anything is possible if you're determined enough." He leaned over and pressed a kiss to her nose. "If we've proven anything this weekend, we're finally admitted we both love you, Hayley. That we don't want to lose you and we're willing to share you if it is the only way to keep by us."

She gestured with her chin toward the door where Max had disappeared. "His family's going to be freaked out about this, aren't they?"

"Maybe? Maybe not?" Noah lifted one shoulder before dropping it. "They're pretty open minded but yeah, this might take them a while to process everything."

Having her own *processing* problems, she leaned in to examine the numerous framed photographs mounted on the wall over the drafting table. There was one of Mr. and Mrs. Moretti when they were much younger, another of the entire family sitting in front of a Christmas tree, a teenaged Max's arm slung over Noah's shoulder right in the midst of them all, a half dozen of Max in a hockey uniform surrounded by a team, more than half of which had a trophy in front of them. There were school photos of his various nieces and nephews, and his sister Jackie with her arm holding hands with her wife, both women wearing beautiful red and gold wedding saris, and another of the two women holding a toddler with dark hair and big dark eyes.

""What if they don't accept it? The three of us?"

"We cross that bridge when we come to it. I think—"

Before Noah could finish, Max bounded back in the room, his energy filling the space. "That was Ma reminding me that I promised to fix the railing on her porch next weekend. And they're going to have another barbecue because it's Sangita's birthday next Saturday, so you guys gotta come."

"Count me in," Noah replied easily.

"I gotta hit the can and then we can discuss what we do for the rest of the day, okay?"

He tossed his phone onto the drafting table, knocking over the single framed photo sitting in the corner, and disappeared into the bathroom.

Hayley straightened the picture then stopped. How had she not noticed this one before? It was of Max and Noah in front of Max's

M&M Construction truck, with her between them, their arms draped around her shoulders. She lifted it to study it closer. She remembered the photo being taken but she'd never noticed how she was grinning directly into the camera while Noah's and Max's gazes were locked on her. She let her fingertips hover over the photo, marveling at the love clear on both their face. "How did I not see it all these years?"

Noah stood behind her, stroking her shoulders. "People see what they expect to see. You saw us as friends, as business partners."

"Why didn't you say something?"

"You were with Darrell. Neither of us were about to interfere with your relationship."

Maybe if she'd seen what was right front of her, she would have dumped Darrell long ago. "How could you stand it? Loving someone and not knowing if they'll never love you back."

"The alternative was not having you in our lives at all. I wasn't about to destroy our friendship. Max was probably the same."

"So," Max returned, rubbed his hands on a towel that he pitched into the bathroom. Where it probably landed on the floor, Hayley guessed. "Who's up for binge watching some Property Brothers? I'll make the popcorn and we can throw it at anyone who complains about the kitchen not having stainless steel appliances or not liking a house because of the paint colors?"

Because Noah was facing her, not Max, she saw his quick grin, a light carefree expression she'd seldom seen. For the first time, she realized his face had been much more expressive this weekend. That the Noah she normally saw was a mask.

They watched three shows before she grew bored and poked Max's belly again. "Did I once mention watching TV was part of my fantasy?" Hayley pointed at the box of condoms on the bedside table "Grab your tack, mister, I want to give you both a blow job you'll never forget."

Gratitude flashed in Noah's eyes. He stood, then sweeping one arm to the side, and clasping the other to his chest, he bowed like one of the old-fashioned swashbucklers. "As you wish."

Which completely melted her.

Until he straightened, and he grinned. "Anything for you, sweet cheeks."

She swatted his ass. "Call me sweet cheeks one more time and you won't be able to sit on yours for a couple of days."

His grin widened. "Promises, promises."

Chapter 13

Max yawned, plopped his ass on the barstool and picked up the coffee Noah slid across the counter.

"You're looking like the proverbial cat who ate the canary," Noah said quietly, hitching one hip against the across from him.

"I think you got that analogy wrong ways round." Max stretched contentedly. "I'd say that pussy sure did love being eaten."

Noah chuckled. "Unless *fuck, holy fuck, yes* was some secret code for a complaint."

Nothing they'd done after he'd returned from his mother's phone call was about Hayley's fantasy anymore. Especially when he'd ended up buried balls deep in Hayley's tight pussy while Hayley blew Noah's dick.

The shower turned on overhead. Hayley was up. He'd been blessed when he met her. Blessed when he'd met Noah too. And now they were in his life, he couldn't imagine life without them. Either of them.

"Do you think she'll stay. Like permanently? Or do you think she still sees this as just a one-time or short term deal?"

Noah considered the remnants of coffee in his cup before answering. "I'm not sure. She's worried about how your family takes it though. She won't want to cause problems for you with them."

"They'll come around. I'm pretty sure," Max said, only semi-confident, but whatever happened he was keeping both Hayley and Noah in his life. Preferably in his house. But how could they convince Hayley to stay if she balked now?

The two men were still considering the conundrum when Hayley wandered into the kitchen.

Max soaked up the sight of her bare feet, and trim ankles. She wore one of his M&M construction T-shirts—it was big enough that she could wear it like a dress, and a pair of his board shorts—she'd cinched the string waist band into a bow. A bolt of need burned in his gut. He wanted this woman. And he'd do anything to have it be long-term, to have her as a part of his future.

He frowned at how she gingerly hitched herself onto the bar stool beside him. "Did we hurt you?"

She accepted the mug of coffee Noah handed her, sipped it then raised an eyebrow in his direction. "Let's say you got a little over-enthusiastic that last time, Moretti. You need to go a little slower next time you jam that fucking big rod of yours in my ass."

"I'm sorry I'm so well endowed." He dusted his knuckles against his chest in mock pride, though her obvious discomfort worried him. "It's a curse of being a male Moretti, but we can take a break on fucking your ass for a while."

"Gee, thanks," she replied drily. "I'm not complaining, but I think I need a day or two off to recover."

Max brushed a kiss over Hayley's cheek before he placed his mug in the sink. If he ever smelled Hayley's shampoo anywhere in the future, he'd immediately remember this weekend. There'd been something more than simple lust in her face last night. More than love too. It had been pure happiness, for herself, for Noah and himself, maybe even relief. They'd ended up falling asleep until almost midnight. He'd woken to the three of them sprawled together, Noah spooning Hayley, Hayley spooning him.

"I promise next time I'll take it easier." Next time. Holy shit. He still hadn't wrapped his head around her agreement to their suggestions. Yet, it had felt so freaking right, so freaking good.

Hayley checked her watch with a curse. "I'm meeting my stager at the place on De Grassi in an hour, but I only have my bridesmaid's dress here. I hope you don't mind me borrowing your clothes. I'll wash them and give them back to you tomorrow."

Noah shrugged. "I've seen people out in worse. Plus it's still a construction site, right? So you don't have to be all dressed up like for the Bay Street types."

"Bay Street." She scrunched her eyes closed. "Fuck. It's Monday, isn't it? After I meet with Amelia I have a meeting with my lawyer about closing the deal on that place out by Bluffer's Park down at the TD Center. I can't go downtown dressed like this. I normally keep a track bag with a change of clothes in my car but—"

"But your car is back at your place," Noah completed.

"Exactly. I know it's a lot to ask but if I give you the keys could you guys run out to my place and drive my car to the site so I can get changed there? It would make it so much easier."

"We could run up to your house," Max said slowly. "But if you leave it to Noah and I, we'll pack your whole wardrobe and move you in with us."

"Max," Noah growled. "No pressure, remember?"

"I'm not pressuring her." Max shook his head. "I'm serious, Hayley. Move in with us. Neither of us want this to be a one-time deal. I love you, and Noah does too."

"I do," Noah agreed.

"I know it's unconventional," Max continued, "But you matter to me, to us. We don't want this to be a one-and-done." He cupped her jaw, his touch feather-light. "We both went into this knowing that you might like one of us better than the other, and we both worried you'd like the other one. This is the best of both worlds."

"Is it? As much as I love you, I don't want to be the cause of problems for you with your family."

"Are you kidding? They'll love you."

"I've seen your mother's shrine in her living room. All the photos of you guys dressed up for your communions and stuff. You can't tell me she would be happy to learn her son is living in a polyamorous relationship, isn't that like a mortal sin or something?"

Shrine was a little excessive. It was a single porcelain statue of the Virgin Mary. Still, it obviously worried her. "Yeah, the three of us living together might make them blink a couple times but they already like you, and they love Noah." He leaned his forehead against hers. "And more importantly they love me, so they'll accept anything that makes me happy. And you, Hayley O'Connell, make me very, very happy."

"You say that now, but mothers get protective of their sons. It might be one thing to say it's fine when a neighbor's kid lives an unconventional lifestyle but you? They'll blame me for leading you astray."

"I'll say it was my idea and let them blame *me*," Noah said blandly.

Max huffed in frustration. "They won't blame anyone, damn it. Here, I'll prove it." He pulled out his phone, dialed his parents and turned on the speaker so Hayley and Noah could hear too. The moment his mother answered, he said, "Hey, Ma, I've got a quick question for you. Hypothetically, what would you and dad do if I told you I'm going to be living with both Noah and Hayley?"

"Max!" Hayley covered her face with her hands.

"Do you mean you're renting her a room or is she moving in with you like a girlfriend?" his mother asked cautiously.

"I mean that she'd be moving in and dating both me and Noah. At the same time." He heaved in a breath and met Hayley's gaze.

"Are you...What...Maximiliano Anthonio Moretti, what are you telling me?"

Oh God, she'd three named him. "I'm asking what you would do if *hypothetically* Hayley, Noah and I lived together. In every sense of the word. Like, as iin we shared a bed. Would you ban us from your house?"

There was a long silence then his mother huffed. "Why would we ban you? You're our son, we love you."

"What about Noah? Would he still be allowed to come over? Or Hayley?"

"Max? What's going on? This isn't hypothetical, is it?"

"I'm just trying to prove a point, Ma." Or maybe he was trying to convince himself he wouldn't lose his family.

"Uh huh." Her skepticism came through loud and clear. "Max, I will always love you."

There was a click as the extension was picked up and his father's voice boomed over the line. "Your mother and I don't care if you're sleeping with the whole damned Maple Leaf team, son, as long as you stay safe and are happy. Now what's going on, Maxie? Because if this ain't hypothetical, you know your mother and I will love you no matter what. Same as we love your sisters."

Max pressed his thumbs against his eyes to stem the tears that threatened to spill. "Thanks, Pop. That's all I needed to know. And give Momma a hug, will you?"

His father harumphed though Max knew it was his harumph of agreement. "Oh, and Maxie? You're still coming over for dinner on Tuesday like you promised your mother, right?"

"Yeah, I am, Pop."

"Good. Make sure you bring Noah and Hayley with you then."

The connection ended and the phone returned to the home screen. Which was probably good because he couldn't stop staring at it.

He cleared his throat, and croaked, "See, they don't have a problem with it."

Hayley stared between the two men, slack jawed. "You really think a permanent threesome would work?"

"We're deadly serious."

She buried her face in her hands for a moment. "I keep waiting for one of you to break down in laughter and yell 'gotcha!' Except you're not going to, are you?"

"No. It's no joke. We both love you. We both want you in our lives permanently and the only way we can do that without making choose is to all move in together." He wagged a finger at her. "And if you're worried about Mom and Pop judging you, you just heard parents promised—"

She held up her hand to stop him. "Max, you said hypothetically. How else were they supposed to respond?"

"In my experience 'get out of my house and don't ever darken the doorstep again' is the usual response," Noah muttered.

Max started, wheeling to gape at Noah. "I thought you said your father kicked you out because you didn't want to work for him."

"He did. It was Patricia—wife number four—who used the 'get out of my house' line when she discovered me in bed with a guy and a woman. To his credit, Chuck didn't agree with her, and told her it was his house and he was the only person who could ban people, especially his son. There was some screaming and plate throwing, and then it came out he was diddling some new woman and suddenly it didn't matter to him if I slept with the whole band. Until he realized I had no intention of going to work for him."

Noah faced her. "As for the Moretti's, Hayley, they are one of the most open, accepting, loving families I have had the privilege to meet." He caught Hayley's hand. "Max is right. We both love you. We don't to pressure you, but we think we can make this work."

"What about kids? Are you wanting kids? How do we handle that?"

He brushed her hair off her face, letting his fingers linger on the tender skin over her ear. "Are you asking if you get pregnant, would we only love the kid if it was ours? Of course not. I will love any kid you have. Mine or Max's. The question is...do you have room enough for the two of us?"

"I've gone on precisely one date with you each. Of course it's too soon."

Max scratched his chin. "I could argue the one date comment considering how many times we fucked this weekend."

"Those don't count." She pointed at Max. "Jack and Jill party last week," swung her finger to him. "Wedding reception yesterday. One date each. And maybe you could count the last couple nights as a date each too. But that's all. I—I—you know what? I can't think about this right now. I'm late. I have to leave."

She bolted from the kitchen, and snatched up her purse from where she'd left it on the stairs.

"Hayley, wait up, I'll drive you home." Max chased after her when she ran out the front door. "You don't have your car, remember?"

She turned and held up a hand, holding him at bay. "I'll grab a taxi out on Queen. Look, I appreciate the offer but I need time to think about all this, okay?"

"But—" Max stopped only when Noah caught him by the arm.

"Let her go, Max. She's right, she needs to process everything. If we push her too hard now, we'll lose her."

Except Max was afraid they'd already lost her.

Chapter 14

One month later

"What are you waiting for?" Amelia's penciled-on eyebrows arched almost to her hairline. Almost every body part on the stager sparkled, from the piercings in her eyebrow and nose, as well as almost a dozen up each ear, to the bangles halfway up her forearms, to the multiple rings on her toes. Her black hair was buzzed up one side and long on the other. She wore a worn Tegan and Sara T-shirt that hung over her usual black yoga pants. Like her eclectic fashion sense, she favored an eclectic decorating style too, choosing comfort over fashion. She and Hayley had butted heads a few times when Hayley vetoed some of her choices in staging her houses. This latest conversation was just one of many they'd had over the last month "Find them and tell them yes already."

Hayley sat at the dining room table in the now-finished house in Leslieville, swirling the extra-large pumpkin spice latte she'd picked up in preparation for today's Open House. "It's complicated."

She'd seen Max and Noah precisely twice since she'd run from Max's house. Once when she'd accidentally run into them right here as they finished up the last of the painting—she'd said hi and high-tailed it out of the house, claiming to be late for a dentist's appointment. The second time had been two days ago at the Habitat Restore location out in Scarborough as they'd loaded a roll top tub into Max's truck. She'd seen them, but they hadn't seen her.

"Honey, all relationships are complicated. But you've got two guys—two really burning hot sex-on-legs guys—willing to make you the center of their universe. Good guys. Way better than your usual type. So again, what are you waiting for?"

She leaned forward and lowered her voice, even though they were the only people in the house. "They want me to be part of a permanent threesome, Amelia. It's not something I can just go jumping into without thinking about it first."

"Gee, let me think about this." Amelia's black fingernails sparkled as she tapped them against her coffee cup.

"Two totally hunky guys who are two of the nicest guys I've ever met," Amelia continued, "four hands, two cocks—and I'm betting they're both pretty hung, am I right?—their focus totally on you and your problem is...what?"

Uh, the fact that threesomes weren't socially acceptable? That they'd garner comments from disapproving neighbours, and no matter how much Max assured her his family would be okay with it, Hayley had her doubts. "Okay, you want to know what I'm worried about? What about my house? I love my house. I've got it set up just the way I want. Max's house is perfect," she allowed, "but my stuff would just clutter his place. And then there's the Moretti's—I know Max says they'd be okay with it, but they'd always look at me as the woman who...Fuck it. I can't do that to him. His family is everything to him. Besides I've been on precisely one date each with them."

"Don't forget the twenty-four hours or was it thirty six, I lost track, you were naked and bumping uglies with them," Amelia added. "I'd say that counts for at least ten dates. Maybe more."

"I'm serious."

"So am I. You've been pining for them the entire month. Moping about, checking your phone and then getting upset that they haven't messaged you the last couple weeks. And how many times have you driven past Max's house, just this week alone?"

Okay, so she may be bordering on stalker territory.

Amelia wagged a finger at Hayley. "You miss them, and don't deny it, chickie. The only one who has a problem here is you."

She couldn't deny any of it. The last four weeks had been the loneliest since she'd moved to Toronto.

"And by the way, you've been on more than a single date each with them. Hell, you've practically been dating them for two years."

"What are you talking about?" That's what Darrell had said too. What had she missed?

"I'm talking about the barbecues at the Moretti's out in Scarborough. The nights you've spent binge-watching Murdoch Mysteries and then there are the movies you dragged Noah to at TIFF the last couple years, and the number of times you've grabbed dinner and eaten with them both. Even take-out food counts, you know."

"We were working on the project houses and were on deadline."

"It still counts. You didn't have to eat dinner with them. But you did. And what about that time you said you went with them to the Taste of the Danforth and Max stopped at every booth to try every type of food? Or the night you guys escaped the crowds at Nuit Blanche? And when Sophie emailed that photo of Darrell on the Jumbotron, who did you call? It sure as hell wasn't me or any of your girlfriends. You called them."

"I wanted a guy's point-of-view."

"No, honey, you trust them more than your best friends." She reached across and squeezed Hayley's wrist. "Open your eyes and see what's right in front of you. They love you, and you love them. Even if it only lasts a year or two. You're getting a chance at love that some people never get their whole lives. Don't throw it away because you're scared."

"I'm not scared."

"Yeah. You are, hon. All these excuses? That's all they are. A smoke screen. Admit you had the best weekend of your life when you were with them."

"I did but—"

"Stop with the excuses already. If you think you need to date them more then date them some more. As for your house, you can always sell it, or better yet rent it. That way you have somewhere to move to if things don't work out, and in the meantime you'd be making more than you're paying on the mortgage.

"Hiding away from them isn't going to help you decide. And yes, I saw how you cowered behind that big-assed F-350 at the Restore. I also saw how you looked at them—you are completely head-over-stilettos in love with them. All you're doing right now is hurting all three of you. So stop your futzing around, and make a decision already. Don't leave them waiting on you to make up your mind. That's just cruel. To all of you."

Hayley considered Amelia's arguments the rest of the afternoon. A dozen couples were waiting on the front step when she opened the door and started the Open House. By the end of the afternoon, she'd collected dozens of cards from realtors, a sheet filled with names and contact information from the hopeful visitors that she could contact about future houses, and best of all had two potential offers coming in later that night.

She locked up the house, and headed home. Only to find herself turning east on Queen Street instead of west toward the Don Valley Parkway. Her hands shaking, she turned off the ignition once she'd parked on the street in front of the beautiful old Victorian. Two huge urns of rust-colored chrysanthemums flanked the front door, several large pumpkins had been placed on each step, in honor of this weekend's Thanksgiving celebrations.

The front door opened and both Max and Noah walked onto the porch as she approached. Both men had circles beneath their eyes, and Max looked like he'd lost weight.

Amelia was right. She was hurting them.

She clutched her purse to her chest and climbed out of her car. "Hi. Can we talk?"

Epilogue

*E*ighteen months later

There was no traffic – car or foot —in the center of the tiny village north of Toronto at four a.m. on Christmas Eve. The massive spruce lit up the street, its red bows adorning the lower branches—tied only as high as the locals could reach.

His breath mingling with the light fog rising from the snow, Max grinned as he pulled Hayley and Noah along the sidewalk. "It's just up here."

Life with Max and Noah had never been boring, Hayley had discovered when she'd moved in with them on Thanksgiving weekend the year before. She'd always known Max was a glass half-full type of guy, but until she lived with him she hadn't fully appreciated his unbounded joyfulness, or his almost child-like curiosity and playfulness. Noah was his balance, who kept him from flying away chasing his latest whim. Noah kept her in balance too. While they'd initially had some issues with each other's boundaries, their unusual lifestyle hadn't presented as many problems as she'd expected.

Max's family were as good as he'd promised, accepting their living arrangements with a casual aplomb. Her family—well, at least they lived far enough away that it wasn't an issue on a daily basis. Her mother hadn't issued her usual invitations for holiday dinners and when Hayley phoned every week, she'd know they'd answer, though her father stuttered to silence when Hayley mentioned either Max or Noah. But their door hadn't completely closed, so Hayley had hope that one day they'd accept her choice.

"Come on, what are you two slow pokes waiting for?" Max rounded the tree, and with a muttered, "here it is, just like he said," disappeared under one of the ribbon-bedecked boughs.

"Come on then, let's see what he's got up his sleeve this time." Noah followed him, holding a branch up for Hayley so she didn't end up with a face full of snow and spruce needles.

Their excitement contagious, Hayley followed. Noah whistled, and when she straightened she understood why.

The branches of the tree swept down to the ground from high above her head, forming a protective canopy. The Christmas lights were muted by the blanket of snow that had fallen overnight. And beneath it all, by the huge trunk in the middle, Max grinned. "It is like a church, isn't it? So peaceful. Like the world outside doesn't exist."

"It's pretty," Noah agreed.

"I agree," Hayley said, not able to help the whine in her voice. "But why the hell did we have to get up and drive all this out here at this ungodly hour? Couldn't you have brought us here at a more reasonable time? Like noon?"

"Because I wanted to give you your Christmas presents somewhere special, but I didn't want to be interrupted by anyone. We won't get the chance to do this privately later."

"You couldn't give us whatever you bought at home?"

"I could have," Max said. "But—"

"—But it wouldn't have the same feeling as it does it here," Hayley finished. "You're wanting to make a memory." Typical Max.

"I am." Max looked so solemn, but the corners of his eyes crinkled as if he were pleased that she understood whatever it was he planned. "I wanted somewhere peaceful, almost sanctified. Somewhere…"

"Special?" Noah suggested.

Max nodded. "Exactly."

With a glance to Noah, Max reached into his pocket, and pulled out two black silk pouches, embroidered in silver thread with each of their initials. "My life—our lives—changed so much when you came into it, Hayley. I love you, and I want to prove that to you." He loosened the strings holding the pouches closed and poured two silver rings into his palm. "We want to marry you. Both of us."

Hayley pressed her palm to her mouth.

"But we can't do that legally. So I figured we'd say our vows to each other here." He lowered themselves to one knee and held up one of the rings. Up close she noticed that the elaborate design he'd had engraved on the outside was actually all three of their initials twined together. "Hayley, would you do me the honor of marrying me?"

"Of marrying *us*," Noah amended. He pulled out a velvet box from his coat pocket and flipped the lid, revealing two white gold bands, one with a large solitaire diamond. Like Max's rings, Noah's had the same initials engraved on the inside "One can be your engagement ring, the other your wedding ring." Like Max, he dropped to one knee.

After a nod from Max, Noah sheld up the diamond ring. "Hayley Elizabeth O'Connell, I offer you these rings as my pledge. To love, to honor and to cherish you always. I promise that I will be there when you need me to be, to listen when you need me to hear you, to hold you when you need to be held." He grinned, "And I promise to find the best marble for your next project without complaining,."

Max snorted. "And I'm supposed to follow that?" He took a deep breath. "Hayley, I love you. I have since the moment I first saw you, and I will until my dying breath. You have made me happier than I thought possible. You have made me laugh when I wanted to cry, get up when I wanted to hide away, and I promise I will do the same for you. I will be your shoulder to cry on, your buddy to laugh with. And I promise I will always keep a supply of chocolate for those days when you need it."

"Damn it," Noah muttered, "I should have used that line."

Hayley fell to her knees in front of them and held out her hand, allowing them each to slip on his ring. The two rings, silver and gold, glinted in the reflection of the tree's lights.

Her turn. Though she hadn't planned to do this here, she knew just what to say. "I love you both. I think if I'm honest with myself I started falling for you the first day I met you. But because I was with someone else, I didn't allow myself to see the real men in front of me. Then you made a fantasy come true, with no belittlement, no patronizing. You listened to what I wanted, and you offered more. So much more. I thought you were crazy when you suggested living with you both. But I was wrong. I can't imagine my life without either of you now.

"Max, you make me laugh on those days when I want to cry. Noah, you are the rock I can count on, to keep me calm when I'm ready to fly into a tizzy. You have both changed the way I see the world, and the way I react to it. You have raised the bar for what I expect in others, and you have both made me a better person as a result. I cannot imagine a life without either of you in it. and, Max, I promise I'll cheer for the Maple Leafs even when they're playing the Senators,"

Noah laughed, "What about when the Senators play the Canucks?"

She stuck her tongue out at him. "Senators all the way, buddy." Then she grew serious again. "I wish there was some way I could really marry you both, but all I can do is pledge to you now, that I will be there for you both. Always. I will love you unless you leave the toilet seat up, then I'll throw you to the wolves."

Both men chuckled, and she thought Max may have blushed but in the muted light, she wasn't sure.

"I will celebrate your triumphs, and comfort you when you don't. But I will never doubt your love. And I will never give you cause to doubt mine." She took a deep breath, wiped the tears now streaming down her cheeks, aware of the tears on theirs. "And I promise that I will raise your children to love their fathers, and I will always show them the love and respect I have for you both."

As she'd suspected, both men blinked, their jaws dropped at almost exactly the same second, their gazes locking in unison where her hand had flattened over her belly.

"You're—you're..." Max stammered, as Noah said, "Pregnant?"

She nodded. "Of course I don't know which one of you is the father, but I know it's one of you. And that's all I really need to know. I will love him or her because we made them together."

"When?" Max croaked.

"Do you mean when is it due? Or when I think I conceived?"

"Either. Both," Noah answered as Max nodded wildly.

"I'm due around the first week of August next year." The anniversary of their first threesome. "And if my calculations are correct, I think I got pregnant during our trip to Montreal."

A week where they'd played tourist and ate on Crescent Street every evening before retiring to their hotel room to make love long into the night. Where they discussed renting out Max's house and buying a new one. A bigger one, with enough room in the back yard for a pool and the German shepherd Max wanted. Ultimately they'd decided to stay where they were.

Noah got a calculating gleam in his eye. "Looks like we need to go house hunting after all, Max. We're going to need to a nursery."

Don't miss out!

Visit the website below and you can sign up to receive emails whenever Leah Braemel publishes a new book. There's no charge and no obligation.

https://books2read.com/r/B-A-NKGB-ISVAC

BOOKS2READ

Connecting independent readers to independent writers.

Also by Leah Braemel

Hauberk Protection
First Night
Private Property
Personal Protection
Deliberate Deceptions
Hidden Heat
Hauberk Protection: The Complete Series

Standalone
Unashamed
All I Need for Christmas

Watch for more at leahbraemel.com.

About the Author

Leah Braemel is the only woman in a houseful of males that includes her college-sweetheart husband, two sons, a Shih Tzu named Seamus and Turtle the cat. She loves escaping the ever-multiplying dust bunnies by opening up her laptop to write about sexy heroes and the women who challenge them.

Reviewers have awarded Leah's books numerous Top Pick and Recommended Reads designations as well as nominated them as Best Contemporary Romance, Best Erotic Romance and Best Ménage and More. Leah has also been nominated as Favorite Author and Best Erotic Romance Author.

Read more at leahbraemel.com.